Appraised
A Stewart Realty Novel
By Liz Crowe

APPRAISED

First edition. May 7, 2024.

Copyright © 2024 Liz Crowe.

ISBN: 979-8224178223

Written by Liz Crowe.

Chapter One

Miranda

August

The text popped up while I was in the middle of teaching my new assistant how to set up a csv file. Really great timing. I was this close to tossing the hapless girl and the computer out the nearest window.

Need a consult.

I grinned at the tingle that hit my scalp. Shutting the door behind me, I ducked out into the hall of my busy real estate office, smiled at a few frazzled looking colleagues and tapped out my reply.

ME: *Address?*

Him: *5124 Pleasant Ridge*

ME: *Nice. New listing?*

Me: *You know it.*

"Hey, um, Ms..... ah... Missus... Landon?"

I slumped against the wall, ready to admit defeat and move on to a much more pleasant project out at Pleasant Ridge with the very pleasant and oh-so-eager Ben Hannover. "It's Miranda, remember? Listen, let's just call it a day. I've got to go give an opinion on a new listing."

The girl—young woman I reminded myself—seemed to be near tears, which irritated me beyond all reason. I bit the inside of my cheek to keep from lashing out and scaring the poor girl—ugh "woman" — to death, cementing my rep as head bitch on wheels in the process. I'd hired her after all. I'd liked her enthusiasm, which had apparently masked an alarming ineptitude with digital marketing. What in the hell was her name? Something really old-fashioned and forgettable.

But my body had shifted gears and I no longer had a single cell's worth of patience, fake or otherwise. "Just do a few more blog posts, stack 'em up through the weekend, like I showed you, okay? We'll tackle the email list on Monday. I'm all set for the open houses. Thanks for that." I snagged my purse and key fob. "I'll text you later, okay? You've got your to-do list, right?"

"Yes, I do." Anna? Amelia? God, I was a horrible person for not remembering. She wiped her huge, watery, blue eyes and smiled, reminding me that she was the sort of stunningly beautiful type that used to intimidate me, back when I'd allowed myself to be intimidated by beautiful women.

I gave a quick backwards wave, my mind already on the consult. Brushing past fellow real estate agents at the downtown Stewart Realty office, I let the grin return in anticipation. My phone bleeped with incoming emails as I fired up my latest German engineering splurge. I'd earned it. This had been the hardest work I'd ever done, convincing buyers and sellers of houses to trust me to guide them through the process, only making money if deals closed.

It had been five long years. All filled with more self-doubt, second-guessing and love-hate of myself than I cared to recall at this point. I shook my head, refusing to revisit it, especially that nightmarish first year. The one thing that had kept me going was the encouragement of the woman who ran the place. Bethany Gordon, daughter of Jack and Sara Gordon who'd owned and run Stewart Realty, was one of the most patient managers in the universe. "Stick to it," she'd say to me when I'd call or text her with yet another fall through or other disaster. "Learn from it. Move on to the next deal, the next set of clients."

I'd earned top producer honors last year, and when her father Jack, now Governor of Michigan had handed me the heavy cut crystal piece of art with my name embellished on it, he'd grinned wide and reminded me how many women I knew would give their eyeteeth to coax him out of his widow bachelorhood. He'd hugged me and whispered, "I knew you could do it. Thanks for sticking it out," into my ear.

"Stop flirting with me, you dirty old man," I'd said with a smile to match his.

"You are well out of my league, madam."

"Got that right, Gordon." I'd waved the applauding crowd gathered at one of Detroit's new bougie hotels for the event, happy that I had indeed stuck it out.

Bethany and her husband, Rick, had hugged me too. "See," Bethany had said. "I was right. You had it in you all along."

The cool thing was, I had that cheering section every day, too. Stewart Realty was hands-down the most successful regional brokerage for a lot of reasons, but the main one was the people who ran it.

I sorted through my issue with a tough seller for a few minutes with Bethany, agreed on a plan of action, then ended the call even as I drove up the long driveway in front of the giant pile of stone and brick that required my opinion. I switched off the engine but kept my hands on the steering wheel, gripping it so hard my fingers hurt.

I was a successful real estate agent. But my life was a steaming hot mess otherwise.

How had I gotten here, anyway?

I had some idea, because a lot of what I was now—assertive, successful and more sexually confident than I'd ever dreamed I could be—was a direct result of steps I'd consciously taken, leaving the old Miranda Landon far, far behind years before. My phone dinged with a text. I glanced down at the device, expecting something deliciously explicit from the man waiting inside the huge house.

But it was from someone else. Biting my lip at the sight of the name on the screen, I swiped it with a hand already shaking in horny anticipation of my afternoon on Pleasant Ridge.

Mike T: *So, it's almost that time of year again... let's make some plans.*

I hesitated, trying to come to terms with the fact that in a few weeks I'd turn forty-five.

ME: *Yes, please. The usual. With whatever surprise you think will make the big four-five extra super special.*

I waited, gnawing my lipstick, as he replied.

Mike T: *I have such a birthday party planned for you in Sin City. I hope you'll finally succumb to my irresistible pull and stay here for good.*

I leaned my forehead against the steering wheel. Memories of the past five years' worth of birthdays whirled and dipped, making my face flush hot.

God help me, how did I get here?

I wanted to answer him but my hands were shaking too much. Mike had been my savior on so many levels. Considering I'd paid the man a thousand bucks the first night I'd met him in Las Vegas and he'd earned every damn last penny, it was beyond ironic that he now begged me with regularity to marry him and move away from my blah Midwest life.

ME: *I'm working right now but I'll call you tonight, ok? I'm looking forward to it, as always.*

But was I?

The concept of hitting my mid-forties kept me up late a lot these past weeks. A few days under Mike's special attentive care would go a long way towards assuaging that stress. God only knew what decadence he'd get up to on my behalf. He ramped it up a notch every year, ever since our first eye-opening encounter.

I climbed out of the car, fluffed my hair, and straightened my skirt before shutting the door. Sensing eyes on me, I sashayed up the granite steps and pushed the doorbell, my body zinging and pinging with eagerness.

"Hey," Ben said when he held the huge wooden door open. "Thanks, Miranda. I know you're experienced with values in this neighborhood. Come on in." He waved a hand, and I entered, smiling at the no-holds-barred opulence of the interior. Huge floor-to-ceiling windows comprised the entire back of the place, with a view out to a small, man-made lake. I stopped, crossing my arms, one hip cocked as if studying the huge, stone fronted fireplace. Ben stood next to me. Our shoulders brushed together.

"It's a bit of a white elephant, even on this street. It's six thousand square feet. Six thousand? What kind of show-off needs that kind of living space?"

Ben Hannover had just turned thirty, I knew. I'd seen his birthday pictures on Facebook. We'd closed a few transactions together in the past and had done our fair share of mild-to-moderate flirtation. By that time, I was deep into my new life—divorced, slimmer than ever, thanks to a hardcore yoga and diet regimen (not eating for the better part of six weeks kick-started that process), and newly aware of my own sexuality thanks to a thousand dollars worth of a total, terrifying whim in the penthouse suite in the Wynn resort in Vegas.

So during a recent closing, I sat staring at him across the expanse of granite table where our clients were signing papers and set myself a goal. I would have Ben Hannover between my legs within three weeks.

It had only taken one.

"I have had the shittiest day ever," I sighed, turning to the handsome, blond, and eager young man beside me. "Do me a huge favor? Shut up and just kiss me."

He grinned, yanked me close to his lean, dress-suited body, and slanted his lips over mine. His hands moved with confidence, now that I'd taught him a thing or five about what pleased me. I liked things slow at first. I wanted to be teased, taunted, kissed. He was an excellent listener and now knew exactly what to do.

But a different sort of urgency gripped me today. I pushed him away and stared at him, both of us breathing heavy. "I need you here." I took his hand and put it between my legs under the skirt. "Now, Ben. Hurry." I could barely hear my words over the whooshing sound in my ears. My skin was like fire as I undid his shirt buttons and slid my hands up his chest to his neck.

"Yes ma'am," he said, hooking a finger into my panties and slipping them down my legs as he kissed me again per my instructions. I groaned and my knees nearly buckled. "Like this," he whispered into my mouth, his fingers moving pleasantly. He tasted like coffee, gum and a slight hint of an illicit cigarette.

"No." I gripped his biceps and leaned on the back of the couch. Gasping and so desperate for release, I could feel it roaring up from the soles of my feet. "Faster." He nibbled the skin between my neck and shoulder, then bit down as the climax approached under his talented fingers, teased, then retreated, leaving me pissed off. I dragged him down to the floor, unzipped his dress pants, and yanked his shirt open so I could run my hands over his torso.

"Jesus," he muttered as I pulled my skirt up and lowered myself down onto his erection, rolling my hips, propping one hand on his chest, the other on his thigh. "God.... yes...." His hiss turned into a low groan as I moved faster, seeking release and not caring how I got there.

Heat rose from the soles of my feet as he reached up under my shirt and popped open the clasp of my bra. His dark eyes were sharp with intent when I looked at him right before the orgasm took me. At that moment, I leaned down and shoved my tongue into his mouth, requiring that connection as my body shuddered and pulsed.

He groaned and tangled his fingers in my hair, his hips moving fast. "God, damn, Miranda. I can't stop."

I rose all the way up off him, observing his handsome face, his near-perfect abs and chest as I used my yoga toned legs and a grip on the back of the couch to help me. He jumped up, the look in his eyes one I wanted. I backed away, crooking a finger at him before I ran into the kitchen and leaned back against the giant, stainless steel topped island, watching him approach.

"Down," I said, pointing to the floor. He went and as he crawled towards me on all fours, his thick blond hair flopping over his forehead, I had a brief vision of myself, of this thing I'd become, this craven, insatiable stranger. The sensation of his lips on the insides of my thigh drove all thoughts of badness out of my head. This was good. This was no less than I deserved. I spread my legs, twined my fingers in his hair and let myself enjoy another orgasm thanks to Ben's lovely mouth.

He stood, sliding his body against mine. "That do, ma'am?"

I nodded even though I honestly felt like I had another one in me.

"Turn around," he muttered into my mouth. "My turn."

I turned, leaned over the island and exhaled as he slipped inside me from behind, even as my body continued to pulse from the monster climax he'd given me. He thrust deep, rolling his hips, gripping mine, pulled out, then shoved himself back in, hard, harder, forcing my hips against the stone countertop.

"Fuck me harder," I said. "God damn it, Ben. You're not going to hurt me."

And Ben, my lovely twenty years younger than my current boy-toy, did as he was told, his fingertips dug into my hips, his breathing rasping and loud. He came inside me with a grunt and shudder. I laid my bare breasts and stomach on the island, letting it cool me as his hips kept moving. Finally, he draped over my back, sweat slicking the space between us, his lips on my shoulders and neck, his whispers of sweet nothings in my ear.

He pulled me up and stepped away, swiping a shaking hand over his forehead. "Damn that was... um... what's wrong?" He blinked and ducked his head, so I had to meet his eyes. I looked away, unwilling to let him share in this tradition of mine. I had no explanation for it, other than the emptiness I now felt, that I always felt after sex no matter how much of it I got. It never failed to turn me into a weak, weepy mess.

"Nothing. That was fun, Ben. Thanks." I walked back into the cavernous great room, seeking a bathroom so I could clean up and cry in peace.

Chapter Two

The next week was a blur of real estate drama at its finest. It never failed. After the first few years I'd spent see-sawing between roaring success and gut-wrenching failure, you'd think I would have learned. The karmic elasticity of this business could kill you—unless you stuck it out, went to bed, and got up the next day, determined that things would change. They almost always did. Whenever I would look around at all the long-timers in my office, I'd remind myself of that fact.

But by this particular Friday, I was limp from a combination of confrontation and fall-throughs.

"God damn it, I need a beer. No, make that six beers, injected directly into my bloodstream so I can forget this week ever happened."

I smiled at the sound of Ben's voice. I'd been avoiding him since our last hook up at his Pleasant Ridge property, not engaging in the usual, unsubtle banter that typically followed our encounters. Something about the way I'd behaved bothered me. It had taken me a lot longer to shed the innate sense of shame I felt right after. Usually a process that took a few hours, a hot bath, some expensive red wine and a full night's sleep. But the next morning I'd woken up sore both physically and mentally, and by the time I got to the end of that day, I was able to admit that if I never laid eyes or hands or anything else on Ben again, I'd be perfectly fine.

I shook my head, not willing to take a ride on the shame train. I hadn't harmed anyone. The guy wasn't married and didn't even have a steady girlfriend. I deserved it. I deserved every luscious, young, over-eager inch of him. And there were plenty of inches to go around. Tucking my hair up in an unruly bun, I stood and stretched, hoping to intercept him as he made his loud, alcohol-needy way past my office.

My office mate was out, probably getting her nails done or some errant body hair waxed off. She'd been the one to introduce me to the concept of my own bare pussy which I'd gotten used to despite the pain required to keep it that way.

My office included a nice big window that I'd spent many an hour staring out of, calculating and recalculating my dwindling bank accounts and burgeoning credit card bills. As if doing so might conjure a winning lottery ticket or sugar daddy.

Today, however, I was in the rare position to be worried about sheltering this year's earnings, despite the recent weeks' worth of bullshit from buyers and sellers alike. It was a good place to be, all things considered. And I was determined to enjoy it. Not to wallow around like I was currently doing, in a stew of annoying, clichéd, mid forty-itis.

A shiver ran down my spine, settling itself low in my stomach. I smiled again, knowing and owning that feeling and getting a pure rush of adrenaline at the realization that it was within my power to do something about it. The sound of Ben's deep laughter propelled me toward my closed door, determined to intercept him. Even as the newly familiar creeping sensation of lameness hit my brain, my phone emitted a sharp bleep, indicating a lead from one of the many internet real estate clearing houses. With a sigh, I grabbed the device and finger-swiped to the app.

Noting an out-of-towner eager to see one of my stalest, most frustrating, over-priced listings, I nodded at the karma, Ben and what he might do to ease my twanging nerves forgotten. I opened my laptop and dashed off a quick email, knowing from experience, and expensive training sessions, that the average internet house shopper demands immediate satisfaction or they'd be on to the next house and the next realtor whose profile popped up thanks to yet more expensive SEO placement.

As I waited for a response, I scrolled through my various social networking platforms, not even realizing I'd been gnawing on my pinky fingernail until I must have hit a nerve, making me wince and glare down at the offending digit. A sharp rap on my office door made me flinch and knock a cold cup of coffee onto my laptop keyboard. "Mother fuck," I muttered, grabbing the scarf I'd worn in that morning and mopping up the drops that glittered on my well-worn keys and praying I hadn't fried whatever electronics dwelling underneath them.

My phone bleeped again, indicating a return message from my internet house hunter. Still wiping the keyboard, I re-opened the phone app and issued a quick, one-fingered confirmation of a showing at said stale listing before glancing up to see Ben filling my doorway. My gaze traveled down his well dressed, firm-bodied form as he slouched, encouraging me. When I met his eyes, the boyish eagerness in their deep blue depths hit me square in the libido. I swallowed, accepting the fact that I felt like a dirty old lady pawing at college coeds, the way my stupid ex-spouse had done.

I waved him away, anger clogging my throat. He blinked and stood up straighter, cocking his head to the side and making him so much more puppyish that I wanted to scream, curse, break something valuable. I shut my eyes, clenched my fingers together in my lap, and willed him out of my universe. When I opened my eyes, the universe had granted my wish. The doorway was empty.

"Hey, Miranda." The sound of my office mate's voice hit my ears. "I know you're in here. This week sucked Satan's ballsack and you need to let it go. Come on. Let's go get a drink. It's a gorgeous day and I know a place where the men who make the best mojitos in town look damn good doing it."

Laughter floated around the hall. Shouts of "I'm in!" and "I'll meet you there, ladies!" made me ever so slightly less pissed. Sure enough, the freshly highlighted mane of blonde hair that framed my office-mate's face appeared. So that had been the beauty-work du jour today. Ashley Prine was twenty-six, slim to the point of emaciated with huge boobs that I would swear were fake, had I not felt them myself at Ashley's drunken insistence once a few years back as we were bonding by engaging in a raucous hot tub party.

At that split second, I wanted my old life back. Complete with cheap red wine, various salads and other gross vegetarian nosh our little group of university couples would throw together at one or the other of our small domiciles. I wanted my husband back. I wanted to be his wife again—the cheating bastard. Because this life exhausted me and was starting to feel way too tawdry. The trade seemed fair at the moment. Which was so patently ridiculous I could barely stand myself for thinking it.

Ashley grabbed my arm and hauled me up out of my slump, smacked my ass, and handed me my purse. "No more work. Drink. Party. Men." She winked. I smiled on reflex, but when she turned to flirt with some of our male colleagues who'd lined up outside our door, I wanted to cry. Especially when I had to acknowledge that I'd slept with every single one of them at some point in the past three years...

"... Of healing," Ashley and my expensive therapist would insist.

"... Of rampant sluttiness," I'd been saying more and more to myself. But I followed her down the gauntlet, tossed a few flirty comments and suggestions of my own—again, on reflex—and climbed behind the wheel of my overpriced vehicle. Ashley knocked on my window. I rolled it down with a sigh.

"Hey, I think Kurt wants to come with. You game?" She gave a nearly imperceptible nod of her perfectly coiffed head. "What's up your ass, anyway, compadre?" Ashley reached into the open window and gave me a quick, painless smack on my cheek. "Do we need this to be a testosterone-free night?"

I shook my head, trying like hell not to cry. It was my downfall, as Ashley liked to remind me. Dudes hate tears.

"Miranda," she said, her voice dropping lower. "What's wrong?"

"Oh, I'm just feeling every single one of my forty-four years and eleven and a half months right now. Someday you'll know what that's like, bitch." I grinned at her, willing my mojo back. I should go out, drink, flirt, maybe get laid.

"Ha! Nope," she claimed, still crouched by my open window. "Look, see this?" She pointed to a spot between her eyes.

"See what?"

"Exactly. Doctor Eyes-and-Tits shot me full of the 'tox today. I look ten years younger, dontcha think?"

I scrutinized her carefully. She looked the same to me, if a bit more perfect. "Sure babe. Whatever. You do know that stuff's poison, right?"

I spotted the new guy in question hovering around between the back door and my car, his dark brown gaze pinned to my friend's ass. I sighed and patted her firm, youthful cheek. "Get off my window. You're getting my paint job all greasy." I flicked her hair. "I'm fine. Meet you at Bola's, right?"

"Yep," she said, rising fast and making me even more jealous at her flexibility. I'd hate the bitch if I didn't love her so much. She tossed her hair over her shoulder. "I think I'm getting the Hill Street listing."

"Holy shitballs, sister. That giant income property? That is awesome!"

"Yeah, it is. So, another excuse. Let's go celebrate." She turned and cocked one perfect hip at her target. He did everything but fall to his feet and start slobbering before Will, one of the older guys in the office, smacked the back of his head.

It had been a long ass week—a long month, really. The market had ramped up, bringing with it big commission checks along with plenty of headaches and heartburn. I suddenly had the urge to laugh like a maniac at the bizarre chronology of my last few years. Year one post-divorce I'd spent in a daze. Year two was more about sulking, crying, feeling sorry for myself. The last three years I'd earned a killer living, exercised a lot, made a ton of new friends and had more sex with more guys than I'd ever imagined possible, all of them younger than me.

I glanced at my hands, now white-knuckling the leather steering wheel. If I looked close, I'd swear I could still see the outline of my wedding ring as if it had imprinted there like a tattoo, a reminder of choices made, promises kept, and then broken with the sort of aplomb reserved for sailors on leave.

Without another word, I hit the up button on the power window, yanked the gear into reverse and screeched out into the busy end of the workweek traffic. It wasn't until I got home did I let the tears flow.

Chapter Three

It was the usual scene by the time I got to Bola's, the new, vaguely Cuban-inspired, overpriced eatery and bar on the corner of Washington and Fourth streets. The place had been some kind of bookstore, but it had failed, thanks to its owner's insistence on pandering to the la-tee-dah-literati and not the people who bought the most books. I would know. I'd been married to one of those piss poor, earnest, know-it-alls for nearly twenty years.

I'd taken a long, hot shower, washing the week's worth of failure off my skin. Used the obnoxiously expensive lotions and whatever else Ashley had talked me into buying a few months ago on a girls spa weekend out to Arizona, slathering it all over my baby's-ass smooth skin thanks to my new addiction to laser hair removal sessions. I was hungry, my brain kept telling me. I'd not eaten a damn thing other than a low fat yogurt and a banana around noon, but I'd been on a mission to hold several deals together. All of which had failed miserably.

It was a buzz writing up offers and listings practically on the hood of my car. But the fall-throughs from all the fakers and porch pissers were, by statistical necessity, also increasing.

Maddening, I thought as I ran my hands down my torso, studying my imperfections with a critical eye. I'd never been skinny. I was almost five foot ten flatfooted and had broad shoulders thanks to my years spent in the pool as a kid and teenager. I'd never, ever been anything less than a size ten, which as I'd been told by the helpful and knowledgeable Ashley was "the new twelve" or something equally depressing.

At the moment, I bordered on "the new fourteen" I supposed, being the ten going on twelve I bounced between, no matter how little I ate or how many hours I sold my soul to the cycle. Ashley had insisted that I'd change my entire perspective on the universe if I tortured myself three times a week with her on those stupid stationary bikes while pumped up dudes yelled at me to go faster. I did like it. It made me forget everything but the extreme urge to jump off the bike, declare everyone in the room full of shit, and stomp out.

"You're statuesque," Ashley always insisted. "Womanly. In perfect proportion. No wonder all the guys tent their tighty-whities every time you walk into a room."

I didn't bother reminding her of the basic simplicity of men. No, I wasn't hard to look at. My thick auburn hair was exotic. I had huge, expressive green eyes and had lived enough years to know how to use them. I had big tits and full hips—my basic shape was, in a word, larger than what was considered perfect in this snake-hipped, ironing-board stomach obsessed world. But I was in an I-don't-give-a-shit-what-you-think-about-my-body-go-work-on-yourself-maybe frame of mind these days. Hell, I might stop doing that damn cycling thing, if I didn't feel so good afterwards.

No, men sensed something else about me—either an eagerness or desperation for their direct, most personal attention. That was what kept them all salivating in my general direction. I put out. It wasn't rocket science.

But I wasn't taken advantage of. Oh no. No man left my bed, or empty house, office, or broom closet, without having satisfied me. I came first. And often. That much was understood, and I hadn't yet met a guy who wasn't willing to fulfill that basic order of operations. I'd spent way too many years thinking I'd had an orgasm at the inept and self-centered hands of my husband. Those days were over.

Thanks to my Las Vegas friend, I mused, letting my mind wander to Mike. The man with the amazing skill set, the beautiful face, the lovely laugh, the generous lips and hands. He was a trained masseur, he'd claimed when we first met. He'd just "relax" me. And we'd see where it took us.

I shivered at the memory of that first week I spent with him. He'd taught me about the triggers, the zones, the way I could use my body to please my partner after I'd been fully satiated. I'm pretty sure that I fell in love with the man that week, but I refused it, rejected it. I'd paid him, after all. He'd taken my money that first time. The other times—all the deeply erotic experiences we'd shared since—were free of charge.

By the time I hit the restaurant door, I'd worked my bad mood into something even deeper. My anger at myself, the world, at all men, had an almost visceral, tangible edge to it. Like I could reach out and grab hold of it, shove into my mouth and chew it.

I took a long, deep breath before moving out of the glass enclosed foyer and closer to the long, concrete-topped bar. This would never do. I'd drink too much, get maudlin, feel even sorrier for my sorry ass self and probably end the night crying.

Dudes don't like tears. Ashley's solemn warning flitted across my brain.

It took a few seconds for my eyes to adjust to the extreme gloom, but I heard her before I saw her, anyway.

"Miranda! Over here!" Squaring my shoulders and attempting to unclench my jaw took a few more seconds. I should have stayed home. "Come on," my friend insisted, loudly. For a split second I toyed with the idea of turning and high tailing it the hell out of here, grabbing a bottle of expensive wine and a cheeseburger and hiding in my house for a few days. If for no other reason than to shake this shitty feeling on my own without trying to pretend I felt like partying with a bunch of younger-than-me, prettier-than-me, hornier-than-me colleagues.

But she'd never let me get away with it. And most days I'd thank her for it. But not today. Today I felt like I could burst into tears, punch someone, scream bloody murder and eat a pint of ice cream all at one time. I gripped the strap of my most recent expensive handbag purchase, shot Ashley a no-doubt sickly grin, and took one step forward into the crowd.

The ice-cold, sticky sensation I finally recognized as an entire pint of beer poured down my chest made me gasp in surprise. "Holy shit," I squeaked out, staring down at my now ruined, once brand new top.

I was positively dripping and somehow my mind couldn't wrap itself around the fact of it, or of the shards of glass scattered around my feet. The guy on the other end of the disaster was staring at my wet boobs. "What the fuck, dude?"

"Oh, I am so sorry," he said in a deep voice, glancing around desperately. "Hey! Can I get some help over here?" He flagged down a waitress. The harried looking woman glanced at our little tableau, rolled her eyes and hollered something over my shoulder at the bar. A white, somewhat clean towel sailed over my head. The girl caught it and tossed it to my assailant. He turned to me and made a few half-hearted swipes at my sticky right arm before making his awkward way up to my shoulder and to my chest.

"Give me that," I muttered, fury and embarrassment making my face white hot. I dabbed at the stiffening fabric, half grateful that this might provide me with an escape clause from this onrushing disaster of a night.

"Here, let me..." the guy said. I looked up to find the man attached to the sexy voice stripping out of his shirt. It was a dark blue, semi-dressy yet purposefully casual style. He had on a black T-shirt underneath that clung to him a pleasant way. But I had no use for his tardy helpfulness or his hotness.

"What the hell am I supposed to do with that?" I had the white cloth clenched in my fist. My new malty perfume filled my nose, making me a little sick to my stomach. The high, screechy sound of my voice made it worse.

"Uh," the guy mumbled, still holding it out to me where it hovered between us. Someone was working around our feet now, sweeping up the glass. I took a second to assess him in my usual way: Tall? Check. Fit? Very. Age? Older than me, if his silvery gray, short cut hair and light beard, and the character lines on his tanned face were any indication. He was indeed hot, even in his trying-too-hard hipster glasses. He blinked in the face of my examination. Then he grinned slowly, still holding that stupid shirt out to me.

It was a moment I mulled over in my head a lot in the coming weeks. I knew it was one of those turning point things you hear about in books. Not too far removed from the one I had on the porch of my professor-suitable bungalow, that warm September evening about five years prior, while I held a quinoa salad covered in tin foil and saw what I saw through the living room window.

I was uncomfortable with positive turning point moments like this one. So I chose to ignore it.

I snatched the shirt out of his hand. He tucked his fingers into the pockets of his jeans, his grin stuck in place, assessing me the same way I'd just done to him.

Men. Not rocket science, remember?

I hooked a finger into the neck of the shirt, tossed it over my shoulder and whirled around as huffily as I could manage and hip-swung my way to the ladies' room. Slamming a stall door behind me, I stood, wondering why I felt so undone. It was just beer after all and I had a shirt from a hot guy to change into, which would likely lead to a lovely encounter because that's just how these things went.

With a curse, I struggled out of the ruined shirt, poked my head out from the stall to determine I was alone. I grabbed and dampened some paper towels, muttering under my breath as I wiped down my front, hoping I'd smell less like a brewery floor and more like a woman ready to forgive a super hot older guy really hard.

I repaired the damage as best I could, stuck my arms into the sleeves of the shirt, buttoning it over my slightly damp bra. I got a whiff of a clean-smelling cologne, or maybe just soap, which would be even better. I hated man-perfume, generally speaking. Reminded me too much of my ex who would not depart the house without a generous amount of it in a cloud around him.

As I dabbed at my flushed face, I gave a brief thought to sneaking out the front door. I could do it without many people seeing me. But I owed a handsome clumsy dude a thank you for the wardrobe rescue at the least. I found myself looking forward to it as I headed back into the crowded bar, sweeping it with my gaze, seeking the man now dressed in his black tee and dark jeans.

He was nowhere to be seen.

"Miranda!" Ashley's voice made me wince and tug the tails of the shirt up to tie them together, resigned now to the evening's previous course.

Chapter Four

S awyer

The longer he sat there staring at it, the harder the trapped lightning bug struggled to escape up the sticky side of the empty beer glass. He was half scorched, half freezing thanks to the too-hot bonfire in the cold Michigan late summer night air. The horizon stretched out like the world's longest bruise. The combined purple, yellow, pink and orange was beautiful and horrible all at once. Especially tonight. Especially since he couldn't pry the image of the woman from the bar out of his head. Or her words, when he'd dumped an entire pint of Imperial pilsner down her silk-fronted boobs.

Your own fault, Sawyer. If you'd stuck around after handing over your shirt, you might have gotten lucky.

But he'd only managed a three-minute wait. He'd stood there like the world's biggest dork in his too tight jeans and even tighter black t-shirt, sans the navy blue, stiffly ironed long-sleeved shirt his teenaged daughter had talked him into wearing.

With a sigh, he tilted the pint glass gently onto its side, watching the hapless insect figure out that the blades of grass now filling its world were a ticket to ride the hell out of a malty death sentence. It toddled onto the grass and gave its handy butt-light a quick test flash. Sawyer allowed himself a quick mental pat on the back for a deed well done. He was about to toss another log into the inferno, blazing for his eyes only when a giant toad snagged the bug on the end of its tongue then hopped away with a croak of satisfaction.

Sawyer sighed, then opened another rich dark stout and drank it right from the bottle, relishing its chocolaty, alcoholic warmth. When he woke, shivering, the fire pit was still smoldering. Groaning at the stiffness in his back and hips, he swung his feet to the grass and sat, trying to sort out what time it might be and whether Emma made it home by curfew. Unlikely. It was par for her course lately and he was damned if he knew what to do about it. At least what to do that he didn't already do—yell, take away her phone, her car, the few freedoms he still controlled. It seemed to have the exact opposite effect anymore.

"Get your own life, dad," she'd thrown at him a month ago, when he'd caught her sneaking in after two a.m. reeking of pot.

"I don't have one, Emma," he'd said, his vision dimming with rage at the sight of the hickeys on her neck. "Your mother saw to that." He'd dropped into a kitchen chair, watching as she sauntered around, drinking water, popping her gum and glaring at him. In that second, he could feel the little toddler girl on his shoulders, or in his arms as he read to her before bed. Heaving a sigh, realizing he was hardly the first or the last parent to think the dreaded "where did my sweet baby girl go?" question, he held out his hand.

"We had an agreement. You broke it. Now you're back to bike riding, and grounded for the next four weekends." He made a "gimmie" motion with his fingers.

"What the fuck ever," she'd muttered, dropping the keys into his palm. He clutched them and grabbed her chin, turning her head so he could get the full effect of what some punk had done to her skin. "I'm still fresh, daddy-o. No one's shoplifted the pooty yet."

"Not for lack of effort, it would seem." He hated himself lately. He'd gone weak in ways he'd never dreamed possible. At one time in his life, a life he'd left behind years ago in favor of a desk and fatherhood and the sort of calmness he thought he wanted, he'd never have put up with this crap from her, no matter he was half responsible for her existence.

Now, his new life was as the mild mannered, nerdy looking old dude teaching housewives and small business owning wanna-be's the ins and outs of profit-and-loss statements at the local community college. When he wasn't getting reamed by hotshot, know-it-all realtors in his other job as a real estate appraiser, or hauling rocks and patching drywall with his buddy, Neil.

He'd leaned against the counter top that he'd installed himself in this over-renovated Burns Park bungalow, trying not to pop off like some kind of eighteenth century landed gentry father of a daughter disgraced by walking alone in the garden with her paramour. Emma didn't move, just glared at him out of her mother's face, her mother's gray eyes snapping with disgust or anger or whatever it was that powered her these days. It punched him right in the soul every time he looked at her. He'd averted his eyes, giving way in the face of her overwhelming resemblance to the woman he'd lost, twice.

"I'm selling this place," he'd said when he'd collected himself sufficiently.

"Fine. I don't care."

He'd blinked, startled when he realized the girl was crying. They stood, separated by way more than a few feet of scuffed hardwood, each stuck fast in their own personal tar pit of misery.

Hold her, Sawyer had admonished himself. You are her father. Once upon a time, you were the only one she wanted when she'd scrape her knee or some kid would push her off a swing on the playground. He'd taught her to defend herself, to be strong, not to take crap off anyone.

His hands shook when he put them on her shoulders. Unable to speak for the giant, sickeningly familiar lump in his throat, he tugged at her. She moved toward him for a moment, then wrenched away and pounded up the stairs instead, her expensive, ugly, heavy boots making ugly, heavy sounds on the exposed treads. He watched her go, shoulders slumping at the sound of the slammed door and the barely muffled scream behind it.

"I know the feeling, Em," he'd said, reaching for the half empty bourbon bottle on the counter.

Now, tonight, he made his slow way back up to the house, opened the French doors into the family room addition they should have skipped, and hit the lights.

"Oh, shit..." a male voice said.

Sawyer acted without thinking, his reflexes kicking in as his mind said "intruder" and "protect." He grabbed a collar as whoever it was tried to scoot past him while simultaneously zipping up his fly. He glared at the kid, holding him tight in one hand, unwilling to look over at his daughter.

"Let him go, dad," Emma said, sidling up to him.

"Go upstairs," he said, trying to make his voice sound like a growl, his entire existence coalescing around the hard reality of what he'd allowed to happen right under his nose.

"But..."

"Get upstairs. Now." He didn't take his eyes off the stupid zit-faced creep, squirming and making annoying noises about "assault" and "lawyers." He gave the kid a shake, pleased when his eyes widened in fear. This he understood. This he could handle.

He pressed the young man up against the closed side of the double doors, making a point without actually hurting him. "Get out of my house," he said, keeping his tone conversational. "Don't ever come near my house again. If I see you here, or smell your muskrat breath anywhere near me or my house or my daughter, you'll need a doctor, not a lawyer. We clear?" He put a bit more pressure on the kid's chest, knowing it for effect and nothing more, feeling a twinge of regret for giving up his old life for one at a desk helping prosecutors build cases against entitled lacrosse bros like this one.

He let go. The kid crumpled to the floor, staring up at Sawyer with the sort of fear that made him feel whole again. He stood, arms crossed, putting the full effect of his six foot five, broad shouldered, ex-cop's body into his "get the hell out and stay out" message. Watching as the future politician, or perhaps smarmy English professor with a penchant for fucking other men's wives, scrabbled for the door knob and threw himself out into the dark front lawn.

He sighed and turned. Emma lingered on the bottom step, tears standing in her eyes. "Are you... hurt?"

She glared at him. "No, Dad. I told you. I'm as pure as the driven fucking snow. Christ."

"Get a shower," he barked, unable to stand it another minute. "Then come downstairs. I want to show you some houses we're gonna go look at together."

"I don't give a rat's ass."

He swallowed the ugly retort. She was like some kind of scary evil demon anymore. And it got worse every day. He took a long, shuddery breath. "Get a shower. Come back downstairs. I got drumsticks."

Her eyes flickered. The corner of her chapped, swollen looking lips lifted. He crossed his arms again, thinking, "point to dad."

"Fine," she said, flouncing up the steps and giving the bathroom door a solid slam for good measure. Slamming doors, he mused as he sat, flipping through the options on his computer, his appraiser's mind already evaluating and tsk-tsking over how grossly overpriced everything was. They are my life's soundtrack.

When Emma appeared, her face scrubbed clean and pink, her dark brown hair scraped back in a ponytail, her eyes bright, he felt something loosen in his chest. Still seated, he held out an arm, willing her to come to him, to let him hang onto her for just a minute or two. She did, lingering almost ten entire seconds before pulling away and rubbing her eyes, closing back in on herself.

"I'll take vanilla," he said, pointing to the freezer. She pulled out the box of her all-time favorite, disgustingly processed frozen desserts. "Sit. Look with me."

She handed him one, and they spent a few minutes thumbing through the listings he'd picked out, smaller houses, smaller lawns, start-over attempts to put the horror of the past few years behind them. When they'd eaten the last bit of chocolate-filled, over-sweet cones, she poured them each a glass of water. He drank his, waiting until she finished to ask The Question.

"So, what did I interrupt earlier?"

She rolled her eyes and got up for a refill. "He wanted a blowjob. I wasn't about to do that, but then you showed up while he was trying to convince me." She shrugged, the gorgeous future woman in her shining through so brightly it made Sawyer's teeth ache. "Gross," she muttered around the rim of the water glass.

He cleared his throat, trying to find words, or even thoughts that might turn into words for this moment.

"I mean, don't get me wrong. I've done it before. He's gross. Not giving blow jobs."

"Oh, uh…" He clenched his fist around the drumstick wrapper. "Well…"

She grinned, then kissed his forehead and ruffled his hair. "I'm kidding. God, you should see your face right now, Daddy-o."

"But he was… uh… had his… um…"

"I was giving him a hand job. But it was mutual. It's what teenagers do. Don't try to tell me you didn't, you know, back in the dinosaur times."

Her extreme bluntness was like someone stabbing him between the eyes with a serrated knife, then turning it. He hesitated. "Okay, well. It's why we got you on the pill." His voice was hoarse. He thought he might very well puke beer and ice cream all over the floor.

"Yep. And don't think I didn't notice the box of condoms you stashed in my panty drawer."

"Yes, well… um…" He wiped a hand down his face. She cupped his lightly bearded cheek.

"It's okay. I'm fine. I'm not doing anything I don't want to do. And when I do want to, I have that giant sized supply of rubbers thanks to you." She yawned and stretched. Sawyer closed his eyes, forcing the images of her with some boy's hand down her pants out of his head. It made him want to put his fist through the wall despite his self-satisfaction with buying her rubbers. "'Night," she said, blowing him a kiss and heading upstairs in her ratty blue robe and thick socks.

Sawyer sat a long time, staring at his tightly clenched fists and cursing his life, before hauling himself up and over to the couch where he'd been sleeping since Helen had died. He pretended he didn't sleep there. Always up well before Emma was as if he'd been in his own bed like a normal person. It was but one of the many reasons he had to get the hell out of this house for good.

Right before passing out, his gut churning with the unwelcome frozen preservatives, he touched his left ring finger with his thumb. Finding the new nothing there, when it had taken him thirteen years to get used to the something, he rolled over and squeezed his eyes shut.

Chapter Five

By Sunday, the predictably unpredictable Michigan weather had turned in an autumnal direction. The gray sky was low, caressing the tops of the trees that already looked slumped and worn out when they'd been vibrant the day before. He had to drag Emma out of her nest of pillows and comforter at noon, bribing her with a trip to a favorite local, over-priced eatery before their tour of houses. He knew he could make one call and get a legit house tour set up with one of the few real estate agents in town who'd actually answer his calls. But he wasn't ready for that step yet.

While he was waiting, he pulled up a file he needed to turn in the next morning. It was on one of those 1950s ranch houses over in Ann Arbor Hills—an area of homes centrally located, close to the University but with huge lots, wide, sidewalk-less streets and more location-times-three juice than any neighborhood had a right to, in his humble, appraiser's opinion. This was a tough one. It had all the charm, class, and potential required for the annoying climbers who were filling in the houses over there like over-eager ants.

On the one hand, the buyers were more than happy to fork over almost eight hundred grand for the pile of potential. It did sit atop the back end of a golf course with an acre of trees on a lovely lot. It had a full, dry, finish-able basement, two-car garage, solid roof. No real issues; other than it hadn't been updated in forty years during the time someone's hoarder grandma had lived there. The place reeked of cat piss, cardboard, and cigarette smoke. The all-wood outer siding was either peeling off, dark green with moss, or missing altogether. It was an affront to his ever-practical sensibilities that some idiot would be willing to pay almost a million dollars for it.

With a heavy, Emma-worthy sigh, he opened the spreadsheet of comps—comparable sold properties in the area. Unfortunately, the only decent ones nearby were two-story piles of over-updated excess.

Not a single mid-century modern in sight, at least in terms of recent closed sales. He'd spent hours adding and subtracting for size, style, location, condition and simply couldn't get the damn number any higher than six hundred seventy-five thousand.

That wouldn't go over well. He actually liked the listing agent on this one. How he'd let the owner's kids convince him to list the thing for that much made Sawyer scratch his head. He knew how the agents at Stewart Realty were trained, and it wasn't to over-price houses even if this crazed seller's market allowed for it. He knew the company's owner, Jack Gordon. Of course it was "Governor Gordon" now, of all things, but the guy was what passed for a scion of industry in this town. He owned the biggest construction company in the region, which was currently run by his son. His youngest daughter and her husband ran the real estate brokerage, and they managed dozens of rental properties.

Frowning, he ran the numbers one more time, consulted the estimate his buddy Neil had provided for things like brand new wood siding and de-stinkifying the place, entered his opinion, saved it and attached it to an email with the address in the subject line. Then he hit "send" to the lender in question with a wince. He could already hear the screaming curses, the callings for his head on a platter, the typical appraisers are idiots messages on his phone and inbox.

He closed the laptop with a firm click, determined not to think about it anymore. It was how he handled things in his life these days. Deal and move on. No regrets. If he spent too much time pondering those, he'd be reduced to sitting in a dark room drinking himself to death. And he had responsibilities. Or at least one of them.

"Emma!" he hollered up the steps. "Get a move on."

The silence that met his ears was typical, but then he heard her slamming things around, so he figured she was moving in a forward direction. He dumped his now cold coffee into the sink and put the mug in the dishwasher, his eyes drawn to all the little dings, dents, and deficiencies he'd have to deal with before selling. Toting up that mental list actually calmed him. The thought of honest work with his hands and tools on this place, if it meant getting rid of it and hopefully the memories it invoked every time he set foot in it, gave him renewed energy.

"All right, let's get this over with," his darling daughter said under her breath as she passed him. He grabbed the keys to his truck, and they headed out. She stopped at the back hall mirror he'd installed there once the addition had been completed, tugging her hair up tighter and running gloss over her lips. He watched from behind her, taking in his own scruffy beard, finger-combed thick silver hair and tired-looking blue eyes. "You're a handsome dude, you know that, right Daddy-o?" She turned and frowned at him. "You should try harder."

"I have no reason to try, hard or otherwise, young lady. Let's go. Grits and eggs await."

"Can I have a bloody Mary?" She shot him a sideways glance.

"You turn twenty-one and I miss the party? No? I thought not. Get in the damn car."

They made it to her favorite restaurant, ate in silence, both of them people-watching and making random commentary on what they saw. He paid the astronomical bill. How a place could charge him almost fifty bucks for two plates of eggs, meat, bread and a little coffee and get away with it many times over, never failed to impress him. By the time he started the truck, Emma was already bitching and asking to be taken home so she could do her homework, or nap, more likely.

"Watch it, kid, or I'll let Neil put you on his payroll," Sawyer said as he headed towards the west side of town and the ranch house he'd had his eye on for a few weeks, not acknowledging her long enough for her to get the message. She shut up and sat glaring out the window. By the time they'd tromped through five houses, glad handing realtors, him giving a fake name for plenty of reasons, he'd had enough. But there was one more to go, and he was not the sort of guy to divert from a carefully laid plan.

"I'm sick of this and I'm hungry."

"How in the world could you be hungry? You ate twenty-five dollars' worth of eggs and bacon a few hours ago." He put the SUV in reverse and draped his arm over the back of her seat to make his way down the long driveway and onto Newport Road. She leaned her head back and turned her face to his. The expression on it was so picture-perfect identical to the one her mother would shoot him when feeling put upon by his insistence on adherence to schedules, he had to slam on the brakes lest he back into oncoming traffic. He sat, staring over his shoulder, his eyes hot and his heart pounding.

Damn woman was never, ever going to leave him in peace.

Finally, he managed to collect himself, reaffirm the reason for this torturous Sunday afternoon outing with his recalcitrant spawn. The final stop was a bit of an outlier. A rare, all-brick story and a half on a road high above Huron River Drive—one of those roads not many people knew about other than those who lived on it, or who did what he did for half his living. It was surrounded by tall trees on a three-quarter-acre lot. The kitchen was dated but usable, the basement dry as best he could tell and one of the bedrooms was on the first floor. Emma could have her own upstairs little kingdom to herself, complete with a fifties-style pink bathroom she'd pretend to despise. Sawyer took his role as the irritant-in-chief for his teenager seriously.

She stared at the brick exterior, her mouth hanging open, and then glared over at him. "I hate it," she said. "It looks like a place where some old lady lures little kids in to cook them in the oven." She crossed her arms over her chest. "I'm not going in."

"Fine." He got out and leaned into her open window. "It's my favorite, just so you know."

"Why? 'Cause it's cheap?" She flipped through the options on her iPad. "What's wrong with it? It's fifty thou less than the cheapest of the other ones. Dead bodies, I'm telling you. They're probably stacked up in the basement."

"Probably," he agreed before straightening up and half noting the name on the Open House sign with its cheerful, hopeful clump of red balloons tied to one end. Without a backward glance, he marched up the cracked sidewalk, taking in the slightly wonky tilt of the front porch, knocked out of politeness' sake, then opened the door.

The usual welcome didn't greet him, either in person or by way of a hollered "come on in" from whatever desperate soul of a realtor who'd sat here all alone for two hours on a Sunday. He shrugged, wiped his work boots on the front rug, and started assessing everything he'd do to the place to make it right. Only a bit of cracked plaster here and there, he figured. No big deal. The living room was cavernous and echoing with a wood-burning fireplace at one end and a big picture window with a broken seal, making the view out to the front yard foggy and warped.

He wandered through the small dining room and around to the kitchen, which ran along the back of the house, galley-style, opening at the other end to a room that would work nicely as his home office. He heard a voice coming from somewhere that he ignored, hoping to take a look and bolt, preferring not to be accosted by the aforementioned desperate host. Once he was ready to make an offer, he'd do it through an agent of his choice, not some rookie hoping to round up Sunday lookie-loos and convert them into buyers.

"You are fucking kidding me," a woman's voice said, raised more than was necessary. "What the hell... I mean, shit, god damn it."

Sawyer frowned. His mother, whom he'd adored, had been strict about cursing. Saying something even as mild as "crap" or "dang" always earned him her most pained, disappointed look and a reminder that cursing was lazy and people who did it were slovenly with the English language. Sawyer's father kept his own cursing for his time in the garage or yard, outside of his wife's earshot.

Emma did it aplenty, of course. But he'd decided that battle not worth fighting in the face of so many others that were. His wife's sailor-worthy mouth had been one of the exotic things about her, at least at first. He sighed, shutting out the woman's ongoing, swear-laden tirade as he peeked into the downstairs bedroom and bath combination. It was about half the size of his current one. Perfect.

As he put his foot on the first tread up the stairs, he spotted Emma in the kitchen, glaring around at its small, outdated appliances and cracked ceramic sink.

"Christ-humping, shithead, fuck noodle!"

Emma's eyes flew open in admiration at that volley from the still invisible agent. Sawyer chuckled and headed up, noting that this bathroom wasn't nearly as dreadful as it had appeared in the photos. It was situated in the hallway between two charming little rooms, both with the dormer windows and sharp ceiling angles typical of a classic cape cod.

A loud cry of frustration followed by the slap of what Sawyer assumed was the back door made him glance away from his perusal of the mosaic tile work on the bathroom floor.

"Oh, hello," the voice said, obviously catching sight of Emma. "I'm Miranda." She shifted into calm Sunday selling Realtor mode pretty quickly. He'd give her that. "And you are?"

"Hi. I'm Emma," his daughter said, an edge of awe in her voice. "Are you married?"

Sawyer turned and stumbled down the steps.

"I mean, because you're gorgeous and awesome and my dad is—"

"What she means is," Sawyer was saying as he rounded the corner into the kitchen. "That I'm... uh..." He froze, his hand out ready to shake, the words "I'm her dad and she's nosy," on his lips.

Miranda stood, her nostrils flaring in shock, her hand on the kitchen counter clutching the phone she'd been swearing into. Without realizing he was doing it, his eyes shot to her chest. The last time he'd seen it, it had been doused in overpriced beer. Emma nudged his shoulder. He clapped his mouth shut. The woman—Miranda—blinked fast and crossed her arms, as if to ward off another splash of booze.

"This is my dad," Emma said from somewhere far, far away. "His name is Sawyer Callahan."

Sawyer winced, and realized his hand was still stuck out in mid air, ignored by the amazing woman who'd brought back his capacity for wet dreams over the last few weeks. She tilted her head. A lock of auburn hair slid from her messy updo, trailing along her shoulder. Sawyer's mouth dried up. He put his hand down and stuck it into his front jeans pocket. Miranda's eyes narrowed.

"Sawyer, did you say?" She addressed her question to Emma. The girl nodded and gave him an unsubtle shove closer to the woman. He put one foot out to keep from falling over himself. Beautiful women, he thought. They'd been the bane of his existence his entire adult life. He sucked in a breath when she took a corresponding step away from him.

"You aren't, by any chance, S. Callahan the appraiser? I mean, that would be a little too perfect, wouldn't it?"

He moved back to stand by Emma, crossing his arms to mirror her, unwilling to go down this road but somehow figuring it for karmic justice. Deciding that to lie now would be a waste of everyone's time, he said, "I am."

They stood there, him trying very hard not to fixate on her tits like a teenager. "If I'd known you were coming, I would have brought your shirt," she said. He noted that she was breathing fast, and color was creeping up her neck into her cheeks.

Emma bumped his shoulder. He frowned at her, then glanced over at Miranda again in time to catch a look of raw fury in her deep green gaze. "No worries. Keep it." He turned, ready to end this little encounter and go home to take a nice, long, cold shower.

"Yes, I will, thanks. I'll probably need it since you just cost me one of my best deals."

Emma shot him a funny look. He sighed. "Go on out, honey. I'll be there in a minute."

"My dad's really cool, Miranda. No matter what he did to your deal," she said over his shoulder before skipping to the front door.

Sawyer clenched his jaw, turned and faced the tall, beautiful, furious woman. She was brandishing her phone at him like a weapon. "You.... you're... fucking....gah!" She whirled away from him. He followed her into the dining room. "Six hundred seventy five? Really? Really." Her face was beet red now. He kept his distance, unwilling to defend himself. Never mind, he was speechless at the extreme bizarreness of this moment.

"Your hipster buyers, eh," he finally managed after she spluttered and cursed at him a minute longer. "That was quick. I just submitted the report this morning." His knees were shaking, but he forced himself to sound calm.

"My buyers, yes. Eager, rich and stupid. My eager, rich, stupid buyers. Jesus, man are you that incompetent or just one of those wanna-be-realtor type appraisers determined to fuck up every other agent's life?"

He let his eyes flicker down her front. Based on his experience with Helen's taste in expensive, understated clothes, he figured her for wearing about fifteen hundred bucks worth of silk and wool and leather. He recalled the German-made sedan in the driveway. "Something tells me you can convince your young, eager, stupid buyers to make up the difference."

She snorted and threw up her hands. "Your appraisal was a hack job, Callahan." The way she emphasized his name made an illicit tingle shoot up his spine into his brain, which provided him with a helpful reminder that he'd gone without sex for over four years. It hadn't mattered much, until he'd seen this woman standing there with her shirt drenched in beer a few weeks ago, thanks to him. And now, here she was, ready to murder him with her bare hands. All the while insulting his intelligence with her typical, greedy realtor accusations.

"Save it for your appeal," he said. "Have a nice day." He headed for the front door, his nerves zinging with something he didn't want to identify as raw, painful lust.

"You haven't heard the last from me, S. Callahan," she called from behind him, a strange catch in her voice. He turned, curious, hoping her body language would reveal something, anything, that might give him hope. But she had that phone to her ear again and was glaring at him. When she saw him staring, she raised her middle finger, kissed it and blew it towards him.

Chapter Six

M iranda
"I don't care what it takes. I want a new appraisal done ASAP."

I watched my assistant's eyes widen, a stack of large file folders containing my month's worth of pipeline-filling held close to her chest. I'd lain awake for hours the night before, fuming and seething. It was a familiar sensation, and one I never wanted to revisit.

Men.

They all sucked.

One of them had seduced me out from under my own goals and ambitions—that of a great novel writer, famous screenplay adaptor, Giantess of Letters—the second week of my second year of college. Knocked me up, married me, sat with me through the messy miscarriage and installed me in his stupid, book-lined house. Making me feel like a dolt for as long as he could, keeping me under his thumb while using his other fingers on other women, lots of other women.

But I'd gotten over him and his years of emotional abuse. Oh yes, I had.

And this one? This one was using his bank-bestowed powers to ruin one of the biggest sweetheart deals of my month.

But I wasn't about to take that lying down.

"Listen," I barked at the hapless lender lady on the other end of the phone line. "I'm serious. This guy is a known incompetent."

"No, actually, he's a known conservative when it comes to Ann Arbor evaluations." Her calm voice lit a spark to my smoldering rage.

"He's a fucking loser. I want another one. I'll pay for it myself."

"You know the underwriter..."

"I know you're keeping this loan in house. My client is your new whale. Order another one." I ended the call without listening to her mealy mouthed response.

"Coffee please." I held up my empty cup. "Put those down here. I need a minute. Alone." I glared at her. She snagged my cup and shut the door behind her. I kicked off my shoes and put my feet up on the messy desk. Using the mouse to move aside a few windows on my computer screen, I revealed the results of a Google search I'd done first thing that morning on one Sawyer Gregory Callahan. He had quite the resume, at least what I could locate of it.

An ex-cop, which I would never have guessed. From Kentucky, which I might have, based on what little I heard of his soft accent the day before. A beat officer for a few years in a little town south of Louisville, then in the big city. He seemed uninterested in promotions even after several citations for bravery, saving various citizens from evil and whatnot. Protect and serve, yadda yadda.

He was married, or at least he had been, and I figured his reasons for moving to Ann Arbor were related to his wife, named Helen, now deceased. Helen Callahan, I had known, which was the one thing scorching a hole in my brain.

Helen Callahan had been my ex-husband's colleague in the English Department at the venerable University that anchored this otherwise boring town. I'd met her once or twice, but she and her cop husband hadn't moved in our impoverished circle of untenured professors and their spouses. She'd been one of those over-friendly women, eager to show how much she was like you, when in reality she was plenty of steps ahead, with her cool, slim elegance. It was like the Queen, pretending to dine with the peasants and enjoy it when, in reality, she was counting the minutes she could escape to a hot shower and a walk with her corgis.

She'd written some book. My ex had dragged me to her stupid launch party—funnily enough, at that very doomed snooty bookstore that now housed my favorite Cuban restaurant, bar, and pick-up joint. That bar where her poor widower had dumped his beer down my shirt.

I tapped my lucky fountain pen against my teeth as I dug back into my memory banks for much more about her. Had that tall silver fox of a hubby been at her side that night? I know I would have remembered him. He was the sort of guy you didn't forget. He must not have been there, I decided before leaning close to the screen to try to determine what, exactly, had led a cop from Kentucky to this Midwest college town where he'd developed a rep for ruining high end deals with his lame ass appraisal skills.

The details were spotty. He was listed as a professor of accounting at Washtenaw Community College, along with his credentials as an appraiser. His name was also attached to HandyMan Inc. as an investor. I knew about that operation. I'd used them for a couple of hoarder house clean-outs. They employed high school drop-outs and druggies or something. All I knew is that they were cheaper than any other company and did a great job and the guy who ran the place, Neil Jensen, was super hot.

I leaned back in my chair, tossing up a ball of rubber bands I kept around for that purpose and catching it again and again, pondering exactly why I wished I knew more about S. Callahan. So far, he'd doused me with beer, disappeared before I could thank him properly for the shirt loan, and tried to jettison a deal where I stood to earn enough to make a major life change I'd been planning.

I studied his head shot from the community college website. It must have been taken a few years ago. He was clean-shaven, sans the fine lines around his eyes and mouth I'd noticed. But that hair, thick, silvery gray, a lock of it flopping boyishly over his forehead, and those deep blue eyes, damn. I shivered and recalled that I'd slept in his shirt the night before, sucking in deep breaths of starch and cotton and what I assumed was the essence of one Sawyer G. Callahan—a bit of saltiness, wood smoke, and ivory soap.

I made a vow to take the damn thing to the dry cleaners and drop it in the mail to him soon after, now that I knew where he lived. Olivia

Avenue was a familiar street in Burns Park. And he lived on the upper side, the tenured professor side.

"Hey, did you see this?"

I turned at the sound of Ashley's voice, grateful for an excuse to stop obsessing over this strange guy with the beautiful eyes and way too many weird connections to me. By the time I looked up from her latest crisis and was headed out to show houses to a newly hired football coach, I'd almost forgotten all about Mr. Callahan.

As I was about to pull out of the parking lot and head towards downtown to pick up the coach and his wife for our three-hour tour, my phone bleeped with a message. I frowned at the unknown local number. Being the good agent that I am, I stuck the device in its holder and swiped my finger across the screen as I waited for the traffic to clear, my mind already formulating which of the million dollar piles of brick I'd sell today. We had four to see this afternoon, two more tomorrow. It was, as we say, a slam-dunk. I just had to not be late, not run out of gas or not embarrass myself in any other unfathomable way.

I need you to call me, the message stated, without any sort of "oh by the way this is..." information.

I looked up to see the line of cars with no end in sight and calculated that I needed about twelve minutes to get where I had to be and had fifteen to make it happen. I hit record to voice my reply. "Who is this, please?"

Mystery number: Callahan.

I sat, staring at his name, until someone waiting behind me tooted their horn. I touched the record button again. "What the hell do you want?"

I screeched out in front of a car, cutting it too close but realizing I'd be late if I didn't watch myself.

Sawyer: I want to buy that house. The cape. From yesterday.

I grinned as I waited at the light at Stadium and Jackson before voicing my reply. "Too late. Offer in hand." A lie. But one he deserved.

Sawyer: You'll like mine better.

I put a hand to my face, hating myself for loving his double entendre. The bastard. Play with me would he? I hit record. "I doubt it."

Call me when you can, he responded.

Cocky shit head.

"Sorry I'm busy," I said, watching as it translated onto the phone screen as a text. "I have a new appraisal to order, remember?" After I pulled into the parking lot of the downtown hotel about five minutes early I sat, my inner real estate agent warring mightily with my inner pissed off yet intrigued female. I touched record again. "I'll entertain another offer. The seller's out of town anyway. Have your agent send it over by six p.m., no later."

As I was walking into the lobby, seeking the guy in the block M hat and khakis in the lobby as we had agreed upon, Sawyer sent me a message that, in retrospect, changed everything.

Sawyer: I want you to write the offer. I'll email you the details. I can e-sign it at end of business today. Have fun selling a house to the new coach. He's pretty demanding I hear.

By the time I was back at my computer and saw Sawyer's offer details, I couldn't stop the grin from spreading across my face.

"Hey, let's go get a mojito," Ashley said, dropping into the spare chair and putting her feet up on our conference table.

"Can't," I said, pulling up my online contracts program and plugging in his details, curious about his willingness to make the offer not contingent on the sale of his house in Burns Park. Surely he couldn't afford that thing on his own now. Unless the dead Missus had had a whale of a life insurance policy. "Money on the table, you know." I didn't look at her but knew she still sat there, studying me. I ignored her, filling in all the blank spaces, sending the file to sgcallahan@gmail and then opening my inbox to find his pre approval, nice and tidy and ready to go.

The office was emptying out now that we'd rounded the corner past six thirty. As I was cleaning up a few loose ends, I felt a set of warm, large hands on my shoulders a split second after I heard my door shut. I let Ben ease some of the well-earned stress out of my shoulders, closing my eyes when he leaned down to touch his lips to my neck. But instead of making me want more, as this move usually engendered, I saw the bright blue eyed face of Mr. Callahan.

I shook Ben off me with a frown. My inner conflict raged. Was I a slut for all this action I was getting? Or was I a strong, independent woman exerting her right to have a healthy sex life? "Sorry. Not in the mood." He dropped into the chair recently vacated by Ashley. "Seriously, Ben. Go on. Go out with your actual girlfriend. I'm busy."

I glanced over at him, noting his pouty frown. That gave me strength. Time to cut this off before he got the wrong idea. "Beat it," I said, training my eyes back on my computer screen. "Sorry," added to soften the blow.

He rose and stretched, then, before I could protest, he took my hand, pulled me up and had his lips on mine and his hand up my shirt.

Don't, my inner grown up woman insisted. *Don't let him. Don't...oh shut up you bitch*, my other, hornier self insisted as I unbuckled his belt. So young, I thought, sighing as he teased my nipples and kissed me in that superior way he had. His other hand found its way up my skirt, making my knees almost buckle with the force of the surge of lust he'd brought on not seconds after I'd been congratulating myself on my self-control.

"Sit," he whispered into my mouth, sliding both hands up my bare arms and pushing me into the chair. "I want to taste."

Within seconds I had one leg draped over his still jacket clad shoulder, the other spread as wide as I could get it as he did that, and some more and then still more until I had to bite back the need to cry out too loud into the room. He rose, eyes and lips gleaming. I did the same, pressing him back against the conference table, stroking him, muttering god knows what at that point, I just wanted to come, again and again and again, and forget that I'd ever laid eyes on Sawyer Callahan.

He turned me around, grabbed my hips and pounded into me, once, twice a few more times until he finished with a long exhale. I took a breath and moved forward, disconnecting us, grabbed a tissue and wiped between my legs. As I was rearranging my skirt and he zipped back up then pulled his tie down from where he'd draped it around his neck. I put my hands on my hips. "Okay, that was great. But it was the last time, Ben."

He grinned and cupped my ass, trying to drag me closer. I pushed him away, a little sick at my stomach for giving in so quickly. How I'd become this craven, needy person I had no idea. But something had to give. "I mean it. No more. You were a ton of fun but I don't think I need to remind you that you've got a girlfriend. No. No more lies," I said, putting my hand over his about-to-protest lips. "I don't care but she might. So go on. Leave me alone."

He grimaced and ran a hand down his too-handsome face. I hated him then, with the sort of bright, visceral, gut-deep hatred only a woman who's experienced the ultimate betrayal can feel. I opened my door, hoping the smell of sex didn't permeate the entire back hallway like it probably already did. "Get out, please. Don't come back."

He lingered, like the needy boy he was, trying to kiss me, to shut the door, to touch my boobs. "Listen," I said, putting his grabby hands down at his sides for the third time. "You obviously don't get it. I'm not into you, okay. I mean, I was into having sex with you. But I've decided to move on." I waved my hand around indicating the office and what we'd done there, more than once, including just now.

He stepped back, shot his cuffs and frowned at his expensive watch. I let him think he was initiating this little break up. It was no skin off my nose. As long as he got the message I was sending. "You're the boss," he said. He chucked me under the chin, stuck his hands in his suit pants and wandered out, looking back once. I shook my head, shut my door and put my aching head against the blinds covering the glass.

My phone was blowing up with messages. My inbox was stuffed full after the brief, pleasant, and final interlude with the office stud. Still damp between my legs, I sat and addressed a few of the issues, waiting for one email. Which finally came about twenty minutes later.

"Ok," Sawyer Callahan said in his message. "Send me the e-sign version and I'll get it back to you. I'd like a response from your seller by noon tomorrow. Thanks."

I did as he asked, then took a look at my phone screen. Mike T. was at it again, teasing out my upcoming celebratory Vegas trip. I stared at it a while, acknowledging how tired I was. Tired of all of this and wanting nothing more than to go home, put my feet up, have dinner with someone who gave a shit about me other than what I could do for them, then go to bed, cradled in that someone's arms. This moment of utter weakness infuriated me. I got up and started pacing my office, mentally checking my bank account balance, my various and many successes in the past five years, my cars, my condo, my lovers.

Because of course that someone was my ex-husband. That cheater. That seducer of co-eds. That egregious, charming liar. I still wanted him. And I despised myself and everything I stood for right then because the one thing I hadn't been able to do was to hang onto him.

My computer made the incoming email dinging sound. I saved Callahan's signed docs, put them together with the signed seller's disclosures and his pre-approval letter and proof of wire transfer into the brokerage's escrow account, a whopping five percent of his offer in earnest money, and shot them off to my seller.

As I waited for the client to acknowledge receipt of the docs, I chewed the side of my thumbnail, tasting polish, smelling sex. Finally I got his "received" email along with a "will respond in an hour."

Silly really. It was a full price plus five grand offer. He had no reason to reject it. I got up and started gathering my stuff, leaving the bulk of the tidying up for tomorrow. As I pulled into the parking garage under my condo building, I got the confirmation email and signed contract back. Smiling on my way up the elevator, already anticipating the hot bath and glass of wine, I dropped my keys on the kitchen counter and tapped out a quick text to my new client: "Congrats. You bought a house."

I left the phone on the cluttered table and headed for the bathroom, humming to myself and shedding clothes as I walked.

Chapter Seven

S awyer
    As he sat holding his phone and staring at the file he'd requested from an old friend at the police department, Sawyer mused on a core tenet. Knowing how to find out whatever you wanted to know about a person put you at both an advantage and a disadvantage.

He sat, sipping his third beer and pondering the records for one Miranda Elizabeth Landon. She was divorced and lived at 102 East Liberty, Unit 550, on the top floor of a converted warehouse in an expensive one-bedroom condo. She had a couple of unpaid parking tickets he'd erased from her record for reasons he couldn't explain. She owed about thirty thou on her mortgage, leased herself a new German car every eighteen months, had memberships at two gyms and a yoga studio. Prior to the condo, she'd lived for nearly ten years in a somewhat ramshackle yet charming Old West Side frame house with her husband, Trevor Landon.

When he'd hit that little bombshell, it had taken him two beers and almost as many hours to calm down. Never mind, it was water under the proverbial bridge. And partly his own fault. Snoops rarely find out things they want to know, his dead mother helpfully reminded him.

Miranda had sold him a house. And he was about to ask her to list his. Why? He had no explanation for this. Of course, she was a pro. She was in the top five percent of all real estate professionals earnings-wise. She was number five at her brokerage, which had millionaire agents in the double digits and handled the bulk of the transactions in this county as well as the surrounding ones. A feat she'd managed after only a few years in the business, after her divorce and a year spent at her mother's place in Grand Rapids, perhaps to collect herself after marital failure.

He sighed and put the phone down. "Hey, Em," he called into the family room, desperate for someone to talk to. "Can you come in here a second?"

The girl slouched into the room, clutching her calculus textbook. "What?" She got an energy drink from the fridge and opened it, not looking at him.

"I bought the house," he said, turning his phone face down on the table between them.

"Which one? Oh wait, that brick one with the ugly kitchen and that hot red-headed lady realtor? Wouldn't it have been easier just to ask her out?"

He opened another beer, not rising to her bait. "So that means I gotta get this one sold." He pushed a piece of paper across the table to her. "Here's your list of stuff to do."

She glanced down at it. "You and your lists, eh, Daddy-o?"

He tried out a smile but gave up on it. "Yeah. Me and my lists." He drained half the brew in one gulp. She picked up the paper and her still-open textbook.

"Got to finish homework. Then I'll start cleaning everything out." He held out an arm. She tucked herself into his side, making his heart slow its mad pace for a few seconds. "I think you should ask that realtor lady out."

He sighed, kissed his daughter's shoulder, and pushed her away. "I don't need dating advice from a teenager. But thanks anyway."

She kept her hands on his shoulders, meeting his gaze with that eerie carbon copy of her mother's. "I love you, Dad," she said. "But it's time for you to get off your ass and go get laid."

He spluttered around for a few seconds, unable to form a coherent sentence. She laughed at him, pinched his cheek the way she used to when she was a toddler, then headed back to her homework.

Oh Helen, he thought, watching her go. You are really missing out.

Of course, she'd likely have missed out anyway, considering.

Sawyer shook his head, unwilling to entertain any more thoughts of that. Which meant he had to banish Miranda too, given the too-strange coincidence of her connection to it.

He finished the fourth beer and switched to water. There was work to be done, and he was the man to do it.

A week later, he opened his email to find a flurry of communication about his report on that cursed mid-century modern piece of grandma-polluted garbage. He downed a huge bottle of water as he reviewed the damage. Sawyer honestly did not care if they ordered one or a hundred more appraisals, praying for a miracle. He stood by his valuation. He always did. It didn't endear him to a lot of realtors in this town, but he didn't care.

When his phone buzzed across the table at the ungodly hour of five forty-five, he grabbed it, noting with a slight tremor of anticipation that it was Miranda calling. "What makes you think calling this early is in any way polite?"

"Nice work," Miranda said, sounding a little breathless. "Really."

"Thanks. I pride myself. For what am I being thanked, by the way?" He sipped coffee, hoping to calm the way his pulse raced at the sound of her voice.

"Good Christ, did you really just phrase that question that way?"

He blinked, reviewing what he'd said and realizing what she meant. He put the cup down with a thunk. "I was well trained by a serious grammar Nazi. So what can I do for you this morning, Miranda?"

"No one will take my appeal. They say you're the best. That your valuation should be taken as God's own word from Her lips or some shit."

He chuckled and leaned back in his chair. "Well, that's what you get when you deal in reality and not in fantasy."

"Fuck you," she spit out. He grinned, unable to stop himself. "No really. Go fuck yourself. And the horse you rode in on."

"I'll try. But the first one is anatomically impossible and the horse thing is just gross."

She stayed on the line. He sucked in a breath and blurted out what had been on his mind for the past seventy-two hours. "Go out with me," he said, closing his eyes when she stayed silent for a full minute. "Hello?"

"Is that a question, a request, or a demand?"

"A question. Sorry if it sounded otherwise."

"Oh, all right then. No. Have a nice day." She ended the call, leaving him staring at the phone, heart pounding, skin tingling, anger rising in his brain. Once upon a time, he'd been the sort of guy who could take one look at a girl and she'd throw her panties at him, even if he were in civvies, at a bar, standing around with his fellow off-duty cops. Then he'd met Helen.

He gripped the phone hard, counted to a hundred, set it down and re-filled his coffee cup before doing a mental reset on the day.

Two hours into various homework-grading and appraisal appointment-scheduling his phone rang. He smiled at the name on the screen and grabbed it up, heading outdoors for some much needed fresh air. "Hey favorite sister," he said, stretching out his lower back and making various mental notes on all the crap he needed to get done to the lawn. "How're things back home?"

"Fine, thanks, says the only sister," she said, making him smile. "Other than the usual managing our parents thing."

"I know, I know. I'll be down in a couple of weeks, I promise. You are a saint."

"No, babe, that's you. You've been to hell and back, and I know it. I can handle this." She sighed. Sawyer could hear her kids carousing in the background. "I do miss you, though. How're things there?"

"I miss you too. Things here are…" He stopped. If had to classify things here, he no longer knew how to spin it if he were being completely honest. "Coagulating."

She laughed. "Okay, well, that's good, right?"

"Honestly, I don't know. It's been a weird stretch of days."

"Got a girlfriend yet?"

He eased himself into a cushion-less deck chair. "What does that have to do with anything?"

"Your daughter told me you might."

"No. I don't."

"So you're selling that house, though, right?"

"Yep. Already have a contract on a new one."

"I don't suppose it's any closer to Taylorsville, Kentucky?"

"No, sorry. Uprooting the teenage menace would take more balls than I can be credited with."

"Fair enough," his sister said. "How is she?"

"Slightly psycho with a dash of always pissed off at me."

"I remember those days."

"Well, I don't." He tossed one of the many walnuts littering the patio out at a passing squirrel, missing on purpose.

"No, you were too busy chasing girls to realize what a horrible teenager you were."

He chuckled. "Okay Touché. How's Jim?" he asked, not caring since he didn't really like his sister's husband that much.

"Out of the country again," she said. "When he comes back, he's moving into an apartment."

Sawyer lurched forward, anxiety gripping his chest. "What? Why?"

"Why do you think? We are oh for two in the infidelity game, my brother. It must be genetic." Her voice broke.

"I will kill him, Laura. No lie. I will get in my car, pick him up from the airport, beat him to a pulp, then dump him into the river." He was pacing the patio now, his heart pounding, the hand not gripping the phone curled into a tight, anticipatory fist. "I never liked that sorry so and—"

"Stop," she said. "I don't need to hear that right now. Hey!" she yelled to someone else. "Put that down right now Eric I mean it. Sorry," she said to him again. "These guys are determined to tear the house down. Missing their dad, or something." She sniffled. Sawyer felt like a million miles of garbage for not being there for her. She'd not liked Helen either and he'd known it, but she'd been deep into her life procreating and house-wifing for the rich banker husband, so her words had meant little to him at that point.

"Hang in, Laurie, okay?" He had a hand over his eyes now, willing himself away from all of this.

"I will. No worries. Honestly. I'm good. But go get that girlfriend. It's been three years, Sawyer. You deserve a little something better."

"Sure. Whatever. Call me, okay? I love you."

"I love you. Talk soon."

He sat for a while, contemplating the landscaping and the too-large house with its echo of his cheating, dead wife. Without letting himself think too much about it, he sent a text to Miranda.

Sawyer: *I want you to list my house. Come over tonight at 6 to take a look and let me know your opinion of the price.*

It took her over an hour to respond.

Miranda: *Why the fuck do you need to know my opinion of the price? I'm sure you've set it already. I'm busy at 6.*

Sawyer licked his lips, pondering the challenge of this tall, redheaded, stubborn, foul-mouthed woman for a few seconds.

Sawyer: *Ok, I do have the value set, but I'm not licensed or I'd list myself. If you want the business, be here at 7:30 p.m. If you don't show up, I'll call Teddy Bishop.* He hit send, knowing in his gut that a woman like Miranda would never in a million years allow her biggest competitor to take a listing out from under her, no matter her unwillingness to meet him here, on his turf.

She didn't respond. That made him smile. For the first time in years, Sawyer felt himself opening up to a new possibility, one that he might very much enjoy.

Chapter Eight

Miranda

I sat in my car around the corner out of sight of Sawyer's house until seven-forty, then got out, grabbed the shirt covered in a dry-cleaning bag and marched down the sidewalk. I hesitated, studying the outside of the flawless bungalow, pretending to be evaluating it with my agent's eagle eye. The damn place could be ripped right out of the pages of Architect's Digest under the "quintessential arts and crafts" section. The huge front porch had two ceiling fans slowly turning and was covered with heaps of mums and other seasonal flora. A modern-looking yet classy porch swing with giant, soft looking cushions completed the perfection.

I hooked the shirt over my shoulder and headed up the wide steps. The number eight hundred fifty thousand was pinging around on the agent's side of my brain.

As I reached for the doorbell, the heavy, cherry wood door swung open. He stood there. He being Sawyer Callahan, the man responsible for my recent bout of sleeplessness. His smile emerged gradually. In a way I was beginning to appreciate, as if he were taking the measure of what was making him happy before fully committing to it. He was dressed in dark jeans, a black t-shirt and socks, which made me stare at his feet. I blushed, noting their size and berating myself for such adolescent nonsense. I held out the shirt.

"Thanks for this," I said, clearing my throat. He took it from me while keeping his gaze on mine. I swallowed hard and swung my tablet around to my front to have something to do with my hands. This guy would not get the best of me. He stepped back, indicating I should enter the foyer.

I did, getting a whiff of lemon furniture polish and paint. I smiled at him, keeping it neutral. "So, show me," I said, feeling the blush before it hit my red-headed complexion, cursing under my breath when his grin turned more than a little wry. "Don't flatter yourself, Callahan. I'm still pissed off at you."

"Fair enough," he said, leading me through the first floor, showing me the magazine-quality décor all the way into the dream kitchen/family room addition he said was done "about five years ago or so, I kind of forget." This he said with a hand to his hair, running long fingers through its silver strands. He gazed around at the cathedral-ceilinged space as if seeing it for the first time, his blue eyes cloudy.

"Okay then, the upstairs," I asked, eager to get the hell out of this house with the ghost of his dead wife wafting around in it. We trooped through the main bedroom suite, complete with a giant soaking tub, two-person shower, granite, tile, and upscale fixtures. I peeked into the two other bedrooms and hall bath, also flawlessly updated. The basement was half finished, with a workout equipment area and an office, plus the storage side with its two-year-old furnace and tankless hot water system.

"Roof's two years old too," he said as we headed back upstairs and to the back patio. The backyard was typical Burns Park. Not huge, but lovely with a classy brick paver patio, recessed two-car garage, the perimeter surrounded by flowers and other expensive-looking landscaping.

"All right then," I said, tapping out notes on my tablet. "I have a good idea of what we're looking at. I'll crunch some numbers and—"

He held up a hand. "Spare me the realtor-speak. You and I both know it will sell for about eight-fifty. List it for eight-fifty. I want the sign in the yard by Friday. You can have one open house. Anything more than that is just you fishing for buyers, and I don't have time for you to do that out of my house."

I sensed my mouth hanging open. He stood there in the semi darkness, staring at me. "Drink?" he asked, before stomping back through the French doors without waiting for my response. I took a breath and considered this possibility, discarding it quickly. But by the time I'd made it back into the kitchen, he had a bottle of wine open and two glasses on the table. It would be rude not to, I reasoned, as I sat at a tall table.

He poured the wine and set the glasses in front of me before grabbing a bowl of pita chips and hummus. I blinked, unable somehow to process this effort he'd made. I lifted my glass to my lips. He held his up between us. Embarrassed, I clinked mine to it.

"To a sale," he said, before taking a sip. I nodded and did the same. "If we don't get a serious offer or two in the first ten days, drop the price to eight twenty-five," he said. "I think we will, though. It's that kind of stupid market." He leaned back and put his long fingers on the stem of the wineglass. I couldn't stop staring at them as he moved them up and down, then in little circles around the base of the glass. My mouth dried out and my ears got all buzzy, making it hard to hear his words.

"Okay, no problem," I said. He refilled the glass I didn't realize I'd emptied already without a word. "I think we will too," I said, for lack of anything better. He drank and smiled again, in that super odd, super slow way. I set my too-empty too-fast glass down again, thrashing around for something to discuss, hiding my discomfort. "How did you get involved with HandyMan Inc? I've used them a couple of times. Nice concept."

He held up the bottle. I shrugged. He refilled my glass, reminding me that he had barely touched his first portion. "I met Neil when I worked for the police department. He was bailing out one of his employees who got picked up mistakenly when a neighbor called about a break in at a vacant house on her street. It wasn't a break-in. The kid had been there working. Neil made quite an impression on me that day." He shrugged. "I do a fair bit of work for him myself, when I can. He convinced me to do the appraisal thing." Sawyer's eyes darkened. "Actually, I think you might be surprised at how many things we have in common," he said, startling me out of my semi-trance.

"What? Other than the real estate market and your under-valuation of it?" I picked up my glass, feeling clever and realizing it was probably just the booze. All of a sudden, it was clear to me what was about to happen. I set the glass down and did my best flirty hair flip. He frowned and looked away from me.

"No. I mean, yes, that but... oh forget it." He got up. I sat frozen in place, confused and on the knife edge of what I recognized was super horny.

"Sorry," I mumbled, half to myself. We stayed like this a while, oddly comfortable, while at the same time utterly awkward. He turned around and leaned against the sink, arms crossed, his blue eyes narrowed as if studying me. "What?" I asked, smoothing my hair.

He opened his mouth, closed it again, opened it, frowned, then jumped up and stomped out of the room. I rose, even more confused to find him waiting at the open front door. "Thanks, Miranda. You can go now."

I stood, hip cocked, still doing my mating dance. His frown deepened as he half turned from me. The thrill that shot down my spine confirmed what I suspected. This lovely silver fox of a man wanted me, bad. And despite my anger at him, there was no denying his appeal. I put a hand on his arm. He jerked out of my reach, his jaw clenching in a way that made me hesitate and doubt my assumption.

Despite this, I reached out and touched the soft gray curls on his cheek, something I'd wanted to do for a while. He closed his eyes. I got bolder, tracing his full lower lip with my thumb. I could honestly say that in the last five years of my random, ill-considered wantonness, I'd never felt so conflicted.

On the one hand, I could easily shut the door and pull this sexy, confused, adorable hunk upstairs to his king sized bed and fuck his brains out. On the other, something in me wanted to kiss him a lot, then leave. Saving the best for later had never been my MO, but for some reason it felt like the right thing at this moment.

He took my hand and let it slide up my wrist to my elbow. His calloused palms rasped intriguingly at my skin. I took a step closer. The night sounds of the neighborhood floated in from the open door, enveloping us in childish laughter, slamming car doors, random snippets of music from the not-far-off student housing.

The porch light came on, bathing half his face in light, darkening the other in deeper shadow. His eyes twinkled, but his lips stayed closed, denying me that sexy, slow smile. I leaned in, my hand still cupping his cheek as I sensed myself shift into autopilot, prepping myself for another one-night stand.

"Stop," he said, taking my hand off his face.

I blinked. We stood nearly touching, so close I could smell the wood smoke in his hair, the wine on his breath. "I know you, Miranda," he whispered, touching my lips with a finger, making me shiver. "I understand what you're looking for. I'm sorry. I'm not interested." He side stepped me and held out his hand, inviting me to leave.

A rush of enraged indignation filled my head, deafening me and making words spill out of my mouth. "You don't know me," I said. "No man knows me. And if you think you have what I want, well," I said, putting my hand squarely alongside his zipper, feeling what he damn well wanted from me. "I think you're mistaken. Or perhaps we just misunderstand each other. It's a shame," I said, giving him a stroke and not missing the way his eyes fluttered when I did it. "I'll have the sign in the yard by Friday." Unable to resist, I kissed him, but lips only despite how badly I wanted to go deeper, longer, much, much farther.

It took me a solid five minutes of sitting in my car, still hidden around the corner, before I could stop shaking long enough to start the engine and head home.

Chapter Nine

As the calendar days flipped over, bringing me closer to the one I dreaded, I had to make a conscious effort not to rip off the head of anyone who came near me, including people I considered friends. Never mind, things were swinging around in a positive direction, work-wise. Sawyer's listing was live, complete with glossy brochures, electronic lock box, website landing page, virtual tours and all the bells and whistles. And I had to admit that my assistant was getting better at her job every day.

My paper files were arranged the way I liked them. Deals now pending were on the left side of my computer keyboard, fanned out so I can see the property addresses at the top of each manila file. Deals in negotiation were on the right. Buyers I was still helping were arranged using an A, B, or C system, based on the seriousness or urgency. My bread and butter—all my listings—were in color coded files next to the buyer ones. Sellers I was courting for listings had their own section, with the letters X, Y and Z corresponding to size and price, "Z" being the million dollar houses that, while nice to close, were sometimes not worth the effort. I could list and close three, three-hundred-thousand-dollar houses a hell of a lot faster. All of this paper was backed up in a fancy new online document system that had a room for each transaction, thanks to a recent company-wide upgrade.

I wasn't what you'd call organized. But had learned to be in order to remain on top of my business. Too bad I couldn't be neater in other things—like my laundry, or my love life.

The fact that Sawyer Callahan's name was on one of the pending files on my left drew my eye, which irritated me as I flipped through them, sipping my first cup of coffee. The fact that he also graced one of the listing files made it worse. The pompous bastard. As if summoned, he sent me a text.

Sawyer: *Where's the sign?*

Me: *I don't install them. I was told it would be sometime today.*

Sawyer: *Why don't you install them?*

God, this man was insufferable.

Me: *Because, genius, they have to be installed with a heavy duty post hole digger thingie so the anchor can go deep enough into the ground to support the weight.*

Sawyer: *You pay somebody to do that? I have a heavy-duty post hole digger thingie. Bring it to me and I'll install it. I hate paying people to do simple jobs I can do myself.*

I rolled my eyes.

Me: *Sorry Mr. Helpful, but the sign company is in possession of all my signs. They bring it. They install it. They leave. Go back to bed or whatever it is you were doing. Besides, you're not paying them, I am.*

I realized my mistake as soon as I sent it. Sure enough, within minutes, I received this reminder:

Sawyer: *Actually, Ms. Realtor Lady, I am paying for it, via the obscene amount of money that will be deducted from my proceeds at closing. They call it a "commission?" Surely you have some sort of system for assigning individual costs to each listing? How do you figure out your net profit on each sale? How do you do your taxes?*

Me: *I have a helpful, very attractive man who does my taxes, Callahan. I don't waste my time doing things that other people are way better at. But thanks for the concern.*

I was leaned back in my chair, clutching the phone and enjoying this exchange way more than I should have.

Sawyer: *Do you date this helpful, attractive tax preparer?*

Bingo.

I grinned and waited a full five minutes before composing this response.

Me: *I wouldn't call what I do with him 'dating' exactly.*

I waited, looking at those words and wondering why I said that. I hadn't even flirted with my tax guy. He was married, and nice. So what I wrote was the truth. I hit "send." Then I got up, leaving my phone on the desk. I had enough to do without worrying about Sawyer Callahan's opinions of my sign installer or tax guy.

At eleven a.m. when I was headed out for a closing and had sent my assistant off to manage a house inspection, I glanced down at my phone. The screen was populated with the usual push messages from NPR, ESPN, and other news sources. There was no message from Mr. Callahan. Shoving aside a knee jerk surge of disappointment, I stuck the phone in my purse, ran color over my lips and headed out. There was money on the table. I needed to go collect it.

By the time it hit four p.m. the office was almost emptied out, typical for a Friday since most of us worked full days on Saturdays and Sundays every weekend. It was why I was taking the Monday through Thursday trip to Vegas for my birthday. Cheaper flights. Barely a disturbance within my business, barring disaster. My somewhat less hapless assistant knew when to reach out to me and when to leave me alone. Hopefully, it would be mostly the latter. I had some serious relaxation on my to-do list.

Ashley bounded in around four-thirty, dressed for a closing, her face flushed with success. We high fived and poured ourselves a bourbon from the bottle I kept on my bookshelf. I was looking forward to hanging out with her before I left. I had a suitcase open in my bedroom already and was going to get on a plane soon that would deliver me to a sensually overloaded set of relaxation days.

"I have a date. Of the blind variety, but not from the app, thank god," my friend said, interrupting my musings.

"What?" When I tried to pour us another one, my friend held her hand over her glass. "Since when do you go on blind dates, Ash?"

"Oh, you know," she said, averting her eyes. "I'm feeling a little anxious about...." She stopped and sighed. "I mean, I'm... I want to..." She blushed prettily.

"Oh, of course. You want a husband and a baby." I slammed back my second bourbon, my good mood shattered. "I can assure you, husbands are overrated."

"I know, I know." She slumped back in the chair. "It's weird, right? I just woke up on Monday, realized I had no prospects and wanted some. So, I called a friend of mine who's been telling me about this guy he knows." She shrugged and got up. "I have a date. We're meeting at the Chop House. Can you, you know, do the thing for me?"

We had a system should either of us decide to go on a date. The other one of us would hang out at the bar of said date locale, until the dating one would send a message, thumbs up or thumbs down. Thumbs down meant we were to intercede, pretend to be drunk, and need a ride or help from our friend so she could escape. Thumbs up meant the dateless one was on her own for the night. We'd had way more thumbs down dates than the other kind. It was why I'd turned to hooking up with guys I knew and not pretending they were dates anymore. Dates, I'd decided, were a waste of everyone's time.

"Sure," I said, putting the bourbon away and turning back to my screen. I could hear Ben's voice booming through the back hallway. He'd been a persistent so-and-so, but I'd finally convinced him I was serious. No more fucking around. But a well-programmed shudder shot through me, reminding me what I was missing when his voice got louder, nearer to my open office door.

I straightened, reminding myself that a twelve-day dry spell of man-bestowed orgasms was a good thing. I had plenty coming to me in my future, very soon and with the assistance of a grown man, not a man-boy. I smiled, turned off the computer, and got up to leave. Ashley was standing in my doorway studying her phone when Ben appeared, winked at me, then moved off down the hall.

I had no words for the strange emotion filling me just then and it took me the entire drive home, a shower, a glass of wine and a change of clothes to recognize it as jealousy. My skinny youthful friend with her fresh young eggs was going to mate. And I, the officially dried up older gal pal, would have to watch. I'd probably have to be her maid of honor. Or matron, or whatever it was that useless sacks of forty-four-year-old divorcees were called.

Stop, I said, staring at myself in the mirror. Just stop that right now. Go out, get the thumbs up and go find a stranger. That will take your mind off your misery. I applied a few more light touches of makeup, did a quick blow out of my hair, decided to leave it natural and slightly curling at the ends before I slipped my feet into my highest designer heels and summoned a ride share.

I met Ashley at the small but classy bar area of the town's best steak house. We ordered two glasses of pinot. Tag team flirted with the cute bartender, then sat, sipping in silence. I sensed the edges of my jealousy poking at me, raking against my exposed nerve endings. I was afraid to say anything to her lest I sound as bitchy as I felt.

By the time I was ready for my second pour, Ashley got up to go to the restroom and a familiar voice made my throat dry up. I turned and saw the man who was stuck in my head like a damn popcorn kernel in my back teeth.

Sawyer had trimmed the beard, making it look more like long stubble. His thick silver hair was a little damp or perhaps had a touch of product in it. His skin looked raw and flushed, like he'd spent the day in the sun. He was wearing the shirt I'd brought him fresh from my dry cleaners after having slept in the thing for a night or two.

"Fancy meeting you here, Realtor Lady," he said, leaning on the bar. I steeled myself against the familiar, Ivory-soapiness of him. "Bourbon, no ice, thanks."

"Not really," I insisted, not looking at him. "It's a small town."

He grunted a response and sipped his drink.

"Sign in the yard?" I knew it was. I'd driven by to check.

"Yeah," he said. "Took the kid forever. But I didn't offer to help. I want you to get your money's worth."

I snuck a glance at his profile. He was a compelling specimen. But he had a lingering sort of sadness around him that I understood and convinced myself that I didn't like. "How's your daughter?" I asked, looking away.

"Oh, you mean that stranger who lives in my house, eats my food, drives one of my cars and cusses me out three times a day? She's fine, thanks."

I chuckled. "I remember being that stranger to my parents." I set my empty glass on the bar, wishing the man had chosen a different place to eat or hang out or whatever he was doing. I wanted him. And I had no intention of acting on it, which was making me antsy.

Sawyer waved the bartender over and gestured to my glass. "On me," he said, giving me what had to be a carefully practiced eye-twinkle over the rim of his rocks glass. I rolled my eyes and nodded at the guy holding the bottle. Three glasses were usually my limit before eating something, and I'd made it to glass three too fast for the second time in this man's presence. "You know, you can't ignore me since we have a fair bit of business to transact in the coming weeks. I'll want to do the inspection on the new house next week. That work for you?"

My mind raced ahead. "Sure." I said, pulling my phone from my purse. "But I won't be there. My assistant will handle it."

Sawyer raised one eyebrow and turned so he was leaning one elbow on the bar and facing me in a definite flirt stance, whether he realized it or not. "Why not?"

"I'm out of town," I said, firmly, pulling memories of Mike and his lovely talents around to the front of my brain to block whatever it was Sawyer Callahan was attempting to do to me. "Annual trip to Vegas."

"Ah," he said, turning back to face the bar. I allowed myself a glance at his dark-trousered rear. "Ladies week in Sin City."

"No," I said, wanting him to know this for some reason. "It's my birthday trip. I go alone. I've done it every year, and have for the last five, ever since my divorce."

He turned his face to mine, too close for comfort, so I shifted back and sipped my wine. Once I'd gathered my thoughts about this topic, I decided to over share. I shot him a look I knew was more than a little saucy. "I celebrated my fortieth birthday and my divorce by hiring a man there to take me to a fancy dinner, and then fuck me six ways to Sunday. I got lucky and found a keeper. We have a standing date. While in Vegas and all that."

"Wow," Sawyer said, not sounding in the least bit impressed. "Quite the renaissance woman." He stood up straighter, dropped some money on the bar and turned, smiling at someone over my shoulder. "Lucky guy," he whispered in my ear before shifting to the side and holding out his hand while I sat, frozen in place again. "You must be Ashley. I'm Sawyer, Neil's friend." He took my friend's hand right next to me and put it to his lips. "Neil's description doesn't do you credit. I have a table reserved in the window. Shall we?"

I moved in super slow motion and watched Ashley's face flush, then saw her smile at Sawyer, then wink at me. "You two know each other," she asked, tilting her head towards me, sitting like a lump at the bar. My braggy nonsense about paying some guy in Vegas to wine, dine, and screw me laying on the ground at my feet, stinking up the place. Sawyer shot me a quick glance, his brows knitted together, his expression an odd mix of unhappiness and anticipation.

"My realtor," he said, putting his large hand in the small of Ashley's back to guide her away. "Have a nice trip next week, Miranda," he threw over his shoulder before guiding my friend away from me.

"How funny," I could hear her saying as she leaned ever so slightly back into him, her dream man, father of her future children, fixer of all things in a house, a car, the bedroom. "We work together."

"Is that right?" Sawyer said as he maneuvered her through the crowd and to one of the premium tables. I watched as he pulled out her chair, smiled at something she said, then sat. He met my gaze. I frowned at him. He shrugged, then focused his full attention on the beautiful woman sitting across from him, like a good date.

I got up and left, figuring this for one of the better thumbs up encounters Ashley would ever have. For a while I stood on the sidewalk, letting the busy Friday night crowd flow around me before I started walking, and found myself in one of the old school, original Ann Arbor bars. Three beers later, I was making out with some guy in the parking lot. When he slipped his sweaty hand up my skirt as he stuck his beery tongue in my ear, I stopped him, stumbled away, and clattered down the street in my too-high heels, wondering where my car was. I could already picture the two of them, Ashley and Sawyer, in bed, participating in a movie-quality love scene.

Chapter Ten

Sawyer

He groaned and rolled over, smelling breakfast even as his brain tried to convince him to stay under another hour or so, to sleep past the looming hangover. But when the pillow he dragged over his head didn't block the odors of coffee and bacon, he gave up, and stared at the ceiling.

If he closed his eyes, he would picture her. The red hair, snapping green eyes, lush figure of the woman who, despite their too-close-for-comfort coincidental circumstances, drove him lately. Made him smile unexpectedly when he thought about what she might say, or do in reaction to something he'd said, or done.

So he kept his eyes open.

That little bombshell of a detail she'd dropped on him the night before, at the over-rated steak house while he waited for his blind date, made him shiver with jealousy. She paid some guy to fuck her, she'd said. A stranger to her the first time, which was so dangerous, he really had no words for it. But apparently he was a guy she met once a year on her birthday, which he knew thanks to his friends in the know, would be her forty-fifth this year. A real milestone. And one the paid gigolo would surely make noteworthy.

He gave up and closed his eyes, picturing her body, her full breasts and hips, the way her auburn hair tumbled around her face.

Sawyer was no saint. He entertained the usual fantasies. But when Helen had died after six solid months' worth of pain, arguments, ugliness, accusations and suffering, some part of him—the healthy sexual one—had shriveled and died.

Until recently, which had prompted him to contact his buddy with the "hot chick who'd be a great first date wink wink nudge nudge," for last night's encounter. Ashley was great to look at to be sure and a fun conversationalist. But he'd not been able to dislodge Miranda's earworm of "I paid him to fuck me," for most of the evening. He'd done his best, turned on his long-neglected charm, but had sensed something about his date that put him off. She had a whiff of desperation hovering around her that reminded him so painfully of his dead wife it made him have to choke back the urge to call her Helen by the end of the evening.

They'd eaten, put away two bottles of wine—one bottle too many—and had ended up making out in the back of a ride share car in the driveway of her small, Westside house. But he'd not been into it and was thankful when she put a stop to it.

"Thanks Sawyer," she'd said, taking her hand off his zipper. "But I should go in now. I don't want you to get the wrong idea about me."

He'd gotten out with her after telling the driver to wait, walked her to the door, pecked her forehead, then turned and escaped before he had to tell her he already had an idea about her and it probably wasn't the one she wanted him to have. He had no issues with women who had healthy libidos and the sex lives to go with them. The fact that the lovely Ashley would have bedded him had he pushed the matter wasn't what put him off. It was her somewhat obvious eagerness for something more.

He was never getting married again, no matter how tempting the offer. He'd done it once, against his better judgment, in order to do the right thing by a woman pregnant with his child. Even after swearing he was not the marrying type.

He sighed and climbed out of bed, unwilling to entertain thoughts of his own lameness for another minute. A long, hot shower later, he sat sipping the coffee Emma had made and watching her noodle around on her phone while she ate. The girl was a great cook and enjoyed it, much to his relief. She left him lists of ingredients. He shopped. She cooked almost all of their meals. He cleaned up afterwards. It was a solid system.

"I have some plans for the new kitchen," he said, pushing away his empty plate and running a hand down his bearded cheek.

Emma grunted, ignoring him. His phone buzzed with a text message. It was from an old friend of his, who also happened to be the state's governor.

Jack: *Yo. Callahan. I need a favor.*

Sawyer: *Since when does the highest boss in the state need something from me? And if it involves fixing some appraisal mess, you'd better ask someone else.*

Jack: *You know me better than that. It's about Miranda Landon.*

Sawyer felt a jolt to his nervous system. What in the name of bizarre karma was this?

Sawyer: *Who?*

Jack: *You know who don't be coy with me. Are you going to ask her out or what?*

Sawyer: *Since when do you care about my dating life?*

Jack: *What dating life?*

Sawyer: *Touché Mr. Gov.*

He waited, pondering his next words, when Jack's message hit the screen like a bombshell.

Jack: *I think you should. She'd be great for you and vice versa. She's an incredible agent but has a distinct lack of self-esteem no matter how much money she makes selling overpriced Ann Arbor real estate. You're a sad sack widow who needs to stop playing at being a celibate monk. Sounds like a match made in heaven to me. Get after it, Callahan. If nothing more than as a favor to a friend.*

Sawyer: *We were once not friends, if I recall. Back when I had to call you Mister Mayor.*

Jack: *Water under the bridge, Officer Callahan. Now get off your sad sack celibate widowed ass and call the woman.*

Sawyer: *Wait. How do you even know anything about this?*

Jack: *Real estate agent grapevine my friend. I am still very much dialed in.*

He paused, then sent a text before he talked himself out of it.

Sawyer: *Do you play basketball?*

It was a couple of hours before he had his answer and he had to spend the time aggressively cleaning out the garage in order to banish thoughts of her waking up in some guy's bed. Good Lord Callahan, he berated himself. You don't like her that much. Why do you care?

Miranda: *As a matter of fact, I did, once. Why? You figure a girl as tall as me must have, right?*

He grinned and downed two glasses of water before responding to her.

Sawyer: *I was headed down to the Y and thought you might want to meet me. A little one-on-one. I could use the exercise.*

Miranda: *That is the most loaded, non-sext I have ever received from a man. Bravo.*

Sawyer: *Get your mind out of the gutter for a half second. Can you meet me or not?*

He stared down at his phone, feeling more like an over eager teenaged boy waiting to hear from the prom queen than a grown man begging a divorced woman to play basketball so he'd have an excuse to be around her.

Miranda: *I have buyers until three. If you're free after that, sure. But don't let me keep you from another blind date or anything.* She included a little winky-face at the end, which made him grin like said teenager. *Also, I've got two showings for your house set for tomorrow morning. 10 and 11 a.m. back-to-back. That work?*

He got to the gym at four, unable to stop pacing around the perfectly clean and ready to show house. Emma had disappeared with her pack of friends for a few hours, with a stern reminder she was to be home by eight p.m. being grounded and all. She'd hugged him before she took off, something she hadn't done in a while.

"How was your date last night Daddy-o? I didn't see traces of a new step mommy around this morning."

"None of your business. You're never getting a step mommy, don't worry." He'd scowled at her smirk.

"Never say never. You're too good a catch. Why don't you go out with the lady whose name is on that sign out there? I like her."

"Get out of here and keep your nose out of my personal life, young lady." He'd swung a pretend punch to her shoulder, which she'd blocked, like he'd taught her.

He dribbled around, shooting baskets, waiting for her to appear. The lady with her name on the For Sale sign in his yard was making him as nervous as a kid on date number one, hoping to get his cherry popped. She showed up twenty minutes late, which made him a little insane. But it was worth it.

"Think you can school me, Callahan," she asked, dribbling around him and going in for a pretty layup. "Think again."

He'd been a little afraid to see her in workout gear, thinking his underused body would go on lizard brain alert. But after a few seconds getting used to the sight and smell of her bare shoulders in the sports bra and sleeveless shirt, he was able to concentrate on beating her. It wasn't easy and they played best two out of three with her coming out on top by a single point, and not the one he'd spotted her either.

They sat leaning against the wall, elbows propped on their bent knees, catching their breath and drinking water watching the next group take the floor for their three-on-three game. He snuck a glance at her profile, which made his mouth water with the compulsion to lick the sweat drying on her long neck while he loosed that torrent of deep red hair from its ponytail holder and buried his fingers in it.

He cleared his throat and looked away when she caught him eyeballing her. She got to her feet, putting her strong thighs on his eye level and held out a hand. He took it and got up, not letting go. They stared at each other for a beat before she grinned, slapped his ass and hollered, "Last one to the Old Towne buys the first round!"

He watched her jog to the exit, then turned and frowned at the rest of the men in the room doing the same thing. She had to be the most perfectly proportioned woman he had ever laid eyes on. She was smoking hot, he had to admit to himself, and she had hold of him in a way he didn't know if he liked.

A wolf whistle sounded as she finished her lap around the two basketball courts. She lifted her middle finger to the room, then ducked out the door that lead to the locker rooms. Sawyer shook his head, finished his water and grabbed his basketball.

"Lucky guy," a voice said nearby, which startled him. He followed her, turning left to the men's shower rooms, already formulating an excuse not to meet her for a beer. But he showered and re-dressed, wishing he'd brought a better shirt, and wandered up Washington Street before turning right, headed for the bar she'd mentioned. He'd spent a lot of years feeling foolish after Helen's funeral. He had no intention of going to that place ever again. But the creeping sensation of foolishness was crowding out his excitement about getting her alone at a bar.

Chapter Eleven

"**Y**ou know what I think," Miranda said, bumping his shoulder companionably. He shook his head and finished his third, ill-considered beer. He'd not eaten since Emma's breakfast this morning and it was going on eight-thirty. He should go home, be a responsible dad and make sure his daughter made her grounded curfew. "I think you like me."

He snorted and set the empty glass down, motioning for the check as he tugged his wallet out of his gym bag. "You think too much," he said, not looking at her. This woman, with the spray of un-concealed freckles across the bridge of her nose, had showered, dressed and emerged him without a stitch of artifice, or lick of makeup, between them. Helen wouldn't go to the grocery without the full complement of foundations and whatever else that littered her side of the bathroom vanity.

"No, no, don't get me wrong," she insisted, waving the bartender away when he appeared and turning to face him so he had the full, breathtaking affect of her cleavage revealed at the v-neck of a thin T-shirt. "I don't mean like I'm your type to date or whatever."

"Whew, that's a relief. I'd hate to have to be the one to break that to you." He leaned on the bar, relaxing ever so slightly for the first time since he'd walked in here and found her sitting, drinking, and watching a baseball game on the tv over the bar. He didn't really like how she made him feel. But somehow, having broken the ice with the invite for a game and now this comfortable, friendly round of beers, he was easing into a place in his head where he didn't feel like he had to guard himself from her. "Since we're well established buddies now," he said, wondering how in the hell this might go and going for it anyway, "Tell me what made you think hiring a total stranger in a strange city to fuck you out of your divorce funk was, you know, safe."

She blinked, tilted her head, frowned, and turned away from him. He sat, rolling the eff-bomb around in his mouth. He rarely used it and wasn't sure why he'd done it now. Even as a cop he'd maintained his ability to not say words that flowed from most of them like water over a cliff. She held up a hand. The bartender appeared.

"My friend and I are in need of something stronger," she said, pushing their empty pint glasses away. "Do you have Jefferson Reserve?" She named a bourbon he'd tried a few times, when someone else was paying, in his typical, tightwad fashion. The guy nodded, pulled a bottle off a mirrored shelf behind him and grabbed two rocks glasses. Miranda took them and hopped down off her barstool. "Come on. I'll tell you all about it. But at a table."

He grabbed both of their gym bags and followed her, forcing himself to look at her bobbing, red ponytail and not the sway of her hips. They sat. She poured them each a small portion and lifted the glass to her nose, closing her eyes and making him break out in a cold sweat at the way she caressed the edge of the glass with her lips.

Oh, for crying out loud, Callahan. This isn't a soap opera. This woman wants a friend. Get over yourself. You're not that appealing, not anymore.

He took a deep breath, sipped his, smiled in appreciation, and set it down. "Spill it, Lady Chatterley. I'm all ears."

"I prefer Madame Bovary, thanks." She leaned back, propping her sneaker-clad feet on the booth bench next to him. "I let a college professor seduce me when I was twenty-six and in my zillionth year of grad school. He was forty. He knocked me up. We got married. I had a miscarriage. We stayed married for another twelve years. I never finished my degree. Instead, I stayed home, washing his clothes, figuring out ways to make vegetables tasty, cleaning his house and editing his great American novel. Then one day, when I walked up to the front door of my friend's house with a salad I thought she might like, I discovered that it was my husband she preferred."

Sawyer opened his mouth to say something, anything, to get her to stop revealing all of this to him. But she held up a hand and kept talking.

"I saw them fucking on her living room floor and I ran. I didn't confront him. I loved him, see. He was my hero, my literary knight in shining armor, always working on a book and never finishing it. Blaming the meritocracy of university life for keeping him down, under its thumb, while he graded shitty undergrad papers." She took a breath. Sawyer remained frozen, terrified she'd put two and two together and realize how close they actually were. "But almost a year and a half after I'd seen my friend's bare legs wrapped around my husband's waist in the middle of the day, a sweet young girl came to my front door in tears. She was in the family way. My loving spouse was responsible. She was only seventeen."

Miranda poured another splash of bourbon in her glass. Sawyer kept a death grip on his. "I took her to a clinic, paid for her abortion and told her to drop his class and never come to my house again. She didn't, to her credit, I suppose." Sawyer watched her toy with her glass, turning around and around on the table.

She sipped and met his gaze. Hers was dry, devoid of tears or even the hint of them. He held up his glass. She clinked hers to it after a second's hesitation.

"Don't give me any credit, Callahan. I only did it to protect him, my beloved, wonderful husband. Anyway," she said, setting the glass down and, to his utter dismay, pulling the holder out of her hair so it flowed and bounced around her shoulders. "We carried on in this way for another few months. Then I found out I was pregnant again at the ripe old age of thirty-eight. It was about that time I realized that I didn't love him but had been so effectively gaslit, brow-beaten, and emotionally demoralized by the man, I didn't think I had any choice but to stay with him." She stopped to take a sip. He waited her out, noting the lack of tremble in her hand. She'd been dealing with this—had dealt with it—for a while now, he realized. She didn't require sympathy. She required someone to listen.

"He wanted to be a dad real bad. He'd been devastated, more so than me, after the miscarriage. I think it's all he wanted from me after a while. So I got up my nerve to ask one of the women in my book group how one might go about filing for a divorce. I hated him by then, but he had me trapped. Or rather he'd convinced me as much." Miranda blinked fast, then swiped at her eyes.

"I knew I had to do something for myself for once and get away from him before I trapped us together as parents." She sighed. "He was this bombastic, know-it-all, showboat of a man. Such a classic college professor type it was embarrassing, watching him prance around in his life, getting away with seducing and discarding coeds while pretending he loved me. He loved himself. I loved him too. That seemed a little lopsided. So I left."

She fell silent. Sawyer waited her out, unwilling to fill in any blanks, knowing she'd get to it in her own time. When she looked down, a tear hit the scarred table top. "It took a minute, but I got myself a great lawyer who got me half of his retirement fund and half the sale of that crappy old west side house that was always falling down around our ears. He was one hundred percent useless in any practical way. I had too many witnesses willing to attest to his infidelity. I even had a statutory rape victim at my disposal. Thankfully, she didn't have to testify. He finally took his lawyer's advice and settled without any of that being necessary." She glanced at him as she turned her empty glass around and around on the table between them.

"And now you know how I celebrated. By looking up what I needed on the internet, paying for it with part of the house sale proceeds, flying first class to Vegas, opening the door in the penthouse suite of the Wynn and meeting Mike." Her green eyes flashed with a sort of energy that made Sawyer hot all over. "Mike taught me how a real man treats a woman. Not as a receptacle, but as a cherished equal. He's....he..." She looked down again.

Unable to resist, Sawyer reached across the small table and took the hand she had resting next to the bourbon bottle. She yanked it away from him. "No, no, I want you to know all of it, okay? You're the only one who does, or ever will."

He nodded, not sure he wanted to be the only one, but figuring he'd set this in motion so he'd best follow through. She took a long swallow of liquor, closed her eyes, and then opened them, punching him right in the gut with the force of her glare. "We did everything, tried everything. Anything I wanted, he would do it to or for me," she said in a clear voice, as if discussing the weather and not her explicit sexual awakening. He gulped. The hand holding his glass shook when he set it down on the table. "Bondage, pain, sex shows, leather, orgies, girls for me, girls for him, guys for us both, you name it, we did it." She gave him a little half smile, but his head was spinning with images and visions and his dick was about to embarrass him, making him glad they were at a table.

"Do you want to know my favorite thing?" She tilted her half empty glass in his direction, then went on when it became clear he was incapable of answering that question. "Sensory deprivation. Blindfolded, but not restrained. Being restrained scared me too much. No, just a soft blindfold as I lay on the bed." She sighed and closed her eyes again.

"He'd tease me all over, not just food and tastes, but odors and sensations on my bare skin. My God, I love that." She shivered. "I like a little pain, not too much. Mike was good at figuring out where my threshold was." Sawyer gulped and shifted in his seat. "And guess what? I love to give blow jobs, Sawyer. I found out just how much that first weekend. I'd done it before, of course. My ex husband liked to come in my mouth or on these."

To Sawyer's alarm, she cupped her full breasts, looking down at them before meeting his eyes again. "He was a fan of the pearl necklace, my ex. But he never went down on me. And I was too shy or scared or impressed by him to ask for it." She dropped her hands back on the table. "Mike ended all that for me. Oh boy, did he. Now, no man gets off in my bed without making me come with his mouth first. And I assure you there have been plenty of men up for that challenge in the last few years." She cocked her head, catching Sawyer off guard. "What do you like, Callahan? Since you know all my secrets now."

"Uh," he muttered, shocked and horrified by how turned on he was right then. It would take him half an hour to be able to get up and walk out of here.

"Oh, I'm sorry. Am I being too pushy? Kind of like you asking me, as if it were any bit of your god damned business, why I hired a man to screw me out of my divorce funk?" Her eyes flashed.

He held up a hand. "Maybe you shouldn't measure your worth by how many men have eaten you out, Miranda," he said, sotto voce as a couple had just taken the booth behind him. They glared at each other a few seconds in silence. "I'm sorry if you didn't like my question. I just assumed since you leapt into this dissertation you were okay answering it."

"You think you know me," she said, her words an eerie echo of that night at his door when he'd wanted to kiss her, to hold her, to ease her out of her brittle anger so badly he'd ached deep in his gut for hours after she'd left. "No one knows me and I like it that way." She started to slide out of the booth. He grabbed her arm. She stared down at his hand, then into his eyes. "Let go."

"You don't have to put a show on for me. Let's just say you're right about one thing." She relaxed. He let go of her arm.

"What's that?" she said, still perched on the edge of the booth, ready to escape.

"I do like you," he admitted, tossing back the last drop of bourbon and pouring another. He was well on his way to drunk, and still had work to do at home. But somehow, right now, it didn't matter. "Sit. Drink. I could use a friend. So could you." He held up his glass. She clinked hers to it.

"Your turn," she said, eyeballing him.

"Oh no. I'm not ready to spill my story yet. I will, eventually."

"Oh, great, you get to remain Mister Mysterio," she said with an eye roll. "What am I gonna tell poor Ashley? That girl is smitten with you, you silver fox you." She winked. He winced. They drained their glasses in silence.

Chapter Twelve

Miranda

The plane rose into the air, winging me closer to my birthday celebration with Mike. I watched Detroit disappear below as the attendant refilled my champagne glass with a smile. The plane banked and pointed itself in a westward direction.

I glanced at my phone screen, taking in the fact that Sawyer's house had indeed been priced well as we'd entertained three offers after just a few days on the market. He'd chosen the buyer he wanted. Then he'd set about negotiating with them through me with the kind of thoughtful practicality that made me like him even more.

"Don't want you to have to head out to the love fest in Vegas worrying about me or my little house sale," he'd said in his deep, lightly accented voice just a few hours before. After our impromptu drunk fest post unexpectedly fun basketball game on Saturday, I'd let him join me in a ride share, and then, to my utter horror, realized I was trying to kiss him in the backseat. He'd peeled me off him. But he was turned on if that giant lump under his jeans was any indication.

The whole thing really was a blur now, thanks to how tactfully he handled me. I sipped the champagne, smiling into the glass.

He'd helped me out of the car, then unlocked my door, all the while making me believe he was going to follow me in and end the day like we should have. But he'd not crossed the threshold, just left me swaying in the doorway, and wanting him so badly I could taste him.

"Drink some water," he'd said. I'd flipped him off and slammed the door in his face. I may have called him something stupid, like "Judgy McJudger Pants," because he'd laughed so hard at one point at me he'd gotten the hiccups. But he would not come in.

I woke up the next morning on the floor of the living room, still dressed in whatever I'd changed into after our one-on-one, mouth as dry as sand, head pounding like a son-of-a-bitch. I'd rolled onto my back and grabbed my phone, tried to focus on sending a text. Then gave up because it made my headache worse and called him before I lost my nerve.

"Hey," he'd answered, sounding sleepy. "You all right?"

"You poisoned me and extracted all my secrets. No fair."

"Nah," he said, making a yawning sound. "All's fair."

"Well, this must be war because I sure as hell do not love you," I said, not sure why that had to be spoken out loud even as I spoke it.

He chuckled, alarming me at the realization of how very much I loved that sound. "You sell my house yet, hot shot?" he asked, changing the subject.

"Probably. I haven't checked my email yet. You have two showings, though, so you'd better get dressed and get out of there. Take the kid with you."

"I know, I know," he said. "It's only eight. I have time. Wanna meet for breakfast?"

"You are insane." And I'd hung up, dragged myself to the couch and passed out for another two hours.

I woke to the sound of loud pounding on my door. "God damn it," I muttered, tripping over shoes and other crap on my way to answer it. I peeked through the hole and got a fish eye view of the one man I did not want to see. "Go away," I said, leaning my forehead on the cool metal.

"I have to be out of my house," Sawyer said. "I don't have anywhere else to go. My realtor is super bossy about it."

I sighed, unlocked and opened my door, then backed away from him. He had a tray of coffee and something that smelled too delicious for words in a greasy bag. He recoiled when I reached for a cup. "Dear God, no. Take a shower. I'll sit out here," he said, casting a dubious eye around my messy space. I flipped him off, but he was probably right. I hit a hot shower, brushed my furry teeth and put on a clean pair of jeans and t-shirt.

When I emerged, I stopped to note that he was humming away in my small kitchen as he tidied things up. I had to let a quick thrill of pissed-off pass through me before I joined him, lest I appear ungrateful. He had two plates of breakfast warmed and sitting on the raised granite bar, and was already digging in to his. I sat with a shrug, unable to stop eating until I'd dredged the last bite of home fries through ketchup and drained my coffee. He had the TV on, tuned to sports, which suited me fine.

I got up and patted my overfull belly, hanging onto his shoulder without really thinking about it as I made my way past him back into the living room. "Nap," I said, hitting the couch. "Come on." I patted the soft leather next to me. "You know you wanna."

He grinned and stood, stretching his arms up and giving me a quick glimpse of skin between his shirt and jeans waistband. "Oh, all right. But I'm setting an alarm. I have work to do this afternoon once I'm allowed back into my house." He fiddled with his phone, then dropped onto the couch with a sigh, stretching his arms out. Again, without really contemplating it, I snuggled into his side, draping my legs over his lap. I was asleep in minutes, lulled by the sound of his heartbeat and the sensation of his arm holding me close.

My phone jangled an hour later, making us both startle and wipe drool off our faces. "Sorry," I said, patting his now damp shirt front. He grimaced, but then favored me with that slow, gradual smile. I grabbed the phone. "Yeah?" I barked into it, knowing it for one of the agents who'd booted Sawyer from his house and onto my couch for a decidedly unsexy nap.

I ended the call after stepping out onto my rooftop balcony to get away from him for a second. "Guess what," I said, unable to keep from yawning.

"Got an offer," he said, now stretched lengthwise on my couch, his bare feet crossed and propped on one arm of it. He kept his eyes closed. "I think my head's going to explode. Do you have any pain killers?"

"Yep," I said, heading into the kitchen and grabbing pills and two big glasses of water. "I used to be able to bounce back after a big night a lot quicker than this." I handed him his water and tablets. He swung his feet around to the floor and took them from me. I stood in front of him, sucking back my water, feeling so completely comfortable in his presence it didn't really dawn on me until it was too late that I was a little closer than could be considered friendly.

He reached around me to put the glass on my coffee table, grabbed my leg and tugged me close, lifting up my t-shirt and flipping open my bra so quick I wasn't quite sure if I was dreaming it. He pressed his lips to my stomach and worked his way up in silence. I did what I'd been longing to do for days and buried my fingers in his thick, silvery hair, moving closer, straddling his lap. Our lips met. Just as I was reaching down to unzip him, wondering how I could get up, shuck my jeans and get back into this position, my phone rang again.

"Ignore it," he said, breathless.

"I can't," I said, tugging my shirt off so he could have better access. "But I will." I groaned when he sucked one of my nipples into his mouth. The room darkened around me as I ground down, cursing all the denim between us.

"Miranda," he mumbled around my other nipple.

I held him close, twining my fingers in his hair, feeling his hips move, knowing it for an involuntary movement and reaching down to fumble with his zipper, eager, awkward, needy in a way that was more emotional than physical. My face felt hot, my skin was on fire as he ran his hands down my back and cupped my ass, pulling me even closer.

The damn phone jangled again. He looked up at me, his blue eyes shining. I put my hand alongside his cheek, pecked his lips and said, "hold that thought, big boy, I'll be right back." I jumped up, grabbed my shirt and the phone and tried to answer one while pulling the other over my bare breasts.

I winked at him, sitting there, sprawled, his chest heaving, his jeans straining the zipper nicely. Then I ducked out the sliding glass door to the rooftop, letting the fall breeze cool my skin as I listened to offer number two on Sawyer's house.

When I went back inside, he wasn't on the couch anymore. With a curse, I ran into the kitchen and found him loading my tiny dishwasher. "Hey," I said, suddenly awkward and embarrassed. "Offer numero dos."

He didn't say anything, just finished up, wiped the granite top where we'd eaten earlier, turned off the water and finally turned to face me. "I'm sorry," he said.

"For what?" I moved closer, eager to maneuver us back to where we'd been before and ready to shuck the whole Vegas trip right now if Sawyer asked me to stick around.

But he side-stepped me, shaking his head and blinking fast. "What?" I demanded, angry now. This was the second time he was putting me off, and there was no good reason for it. "You started it," I reminded him.

"I know, I know," he said, shaking his head so hard a lock of silver hair flopped over one eye. I reached over and brushed it back, letting my fingertips trail down his cheek to his lips. He grabbed my hand, staring at me as if I'd just run over his dog. "What happened to the baby, Miranda?" I stared at him, trying to process what he was asking me. "You were pregnant when you got your divorce."

I moved away from him slowly, crossing my arms, sensing myself close up again in the face of his judgmental bullshit. "What difference does it make?" I asked, my voice shaking. "You won't fuck me if I had an abortion, or what?"

He sucked in a breath. "I didn't assume—"

"Yes, you did. And now you can go." I marched to the door and opened it, using my arm to indicate politely which way he should go to get the hell out of my life. He stood, staring at me for a few seconds, then his shoulders slumped and he grabbed his keys off the small table.

I watched him, trembling with regret, but knowing I couldn't let another man into my life, not this way, not this man with his presumptions and over-tidy ways. No matter how badly I wanted him. He leaned in to kiss me. I averted my face.

"I'll email you the offers," I said. "Thanks for the food." He opened his mouth to speak. I shut the door in his face.

Chapter Thirteen

I did sell his damn house three times over. But despite the temptation of it, I'd steered clear of any actual contact with him, only talking out the offers on the phone then having him e-sign the one he wanted. Always claiming I had buyers or some nonsense when all I really did was sit around and drink weak tea as I tried to remember everything I'd told the man. And to forget how close I'd come to letting him into my bed.

Ashley was wearing me out, trying to get info about him. I kept insisting that I knew nothing other than the fact that he was a tough, to the point negotiator, and a neat freak. I figured she'd managed to bed him. Not many men were able to resist her one-two-three punch of gorgeous, hot, and successful. I resisted the impulse to ask her how he was, what he liked, if he were generous or selfish between the sheets.

So here I was, a couple of surprise deals under my belt, a new friend who didn't want in my pants, apparently whom I trusted more than anyone, considering I had told him more than I'd told anyone, ever. Only a few hours from another birthday in the arms of my once paid for, now eager lover, Mike.

I leaned my head against the cool window, staring at the message from Sawyer again, about the "love fest" and sensing something in me release a little fact to my brain—one that I didn't really want to acknowledge—about how much I wished that he were the one I was going to celebrate with.

No, Miranda. None of that. Sawyer Callahan is not for you. He's as damaged as you are. You don't need that in your life. Besides, by the time Mike is done with you, you'll have forgotten all about him.

I slept. And when I woke, we were touching down at McCarran Airport. I deplaned, found my luggage and walked out into the dry heat, grinning wide at the sight of him, of Mike, his six foot seven inch heavily muscled, mocha-skinned frame leaning against his Porsche. He tossed my bag into the back, grabbed me and kissed me so hard I saw stars. I wrapped my arms around his neck, broke the kiss, buried my face in his chest, and sobbed.

"Hey, hey, what's all this?" he said, peeling me off him and leaning down to meet my eyes. "No crying on a birthday. It's against the rules." He opened the passenger's side door, handed me in and we drove down to the brightly lit Strip in silence, his hand on my thigh, my head on his shoulder.

Once at the hotel where he both lived and worked, he used his keycard to gain access to the topmost floor. Then he loomed over me as we raced up the middle of the building, his hands running up and down my arms, his full lips teasing mine. I barely remember the door opening, us stumbling into the suite, shedding clothes as we went. Music played. Ambient light from the open curtains across the full glass expanse of one wall gave the room a magical glow. I sensed myself falling into this again, this spell of unreality that I didn't realize I'd missed.

Mike scooped me up with little effort, kissing me the entire time, then laid me on the soft, white-sheeted bed. When he took his lips off mine and propped himself on one elbow, I took his other hand and pressed it to my face. "I missed you," I said, meaning it, adoring the way our skin glowed in the lights from the Vegas night shining through the window. He smiled, traced my lips with a finger, kissed me again, then leaned back.

"I have a surprise for you," he whispered, cupping one of my bare breasts and teasing that nipple just enough to make me shiver. "But it can wait, if you'd rather get right to the early celebrations." He kissed his way up my neck, sliding his hands down my waist and around to grab my ass, pulling me close to his body. "Mmmm..." he said as I draped my leg over his hip and angled just so, wanting him inside me more than I wanted to be surprised.

But something was off. We both sensed it. Mike frowned and rolled onto his side, propped up on his elbow, and stared at me.

"What? I don't do it for you anymore?" Tears hovered, and I could sense myself on the verge of sobbing yet again.

Stupid Callahan.

But yeah, it was him. He was stuck in my brain like that damned popcorn kernel again.

"Hang on," Mike said, rolling to the bedside table and then back with two things in his hands. I smiled at one—a tube of my favorite lube. A necessity that he'd planned for. But at the sight of the other thing, I blinked fast, my brain denying its existence. "I was going to wait, but it seems like now is as good a time as any."

"Is that what I think it is?" pointing at the distinctive, square, distinctive blue-green jeweler's box.

"It might be," he said.

"No. Don't," I said, putting my hand over his when he went to open it. "Not now." I put the ring box on my bedside table, took the lube, and grinned at him. "Fucking first. Serious things later."

"I don't get you sometimes," Mike said on our last morning as we shared coffee and croissants on the balcony outside his suite. He was dressed in a suit, headed off for his day job as real estate manager for several casino moguls. He had to have the things tailored, given the breadth of his shoulders and the length of his legs. The effect was mouth-watering, I had to admit, as I put my bare foot on his crotch under the table. He frowned and pushed it to the floor. "I know you feel the same way about me. I also know you don't have a damn thing tying you down in Michigan. Just a job that you can easily pick up here once I hand you a few leads."

He leaned forward, grabbing my left hand and putting the ring he'd tried to give me the night before back in my palm. "I adore you, Miranda. I want you to live here, with me, as my wife."

I stared down at it, an impressive display of platinum and flawless diamonds. It sparkled when the sunlight hit it just right, making me blink and close my fingers over it. I'd never felt more unsure and yet sure about anything in my life.

"I told you before, Mike. I'm never marrying again." I put the ring on the white tablecloth between us. "I will consider moving out here, though."

"You say that every year," he said, his deep brown eyes full of hurt. He tucked a strand of my hair behind my ear. "And then you leave and I don't hear from you until it's time to celebrate a birthday again." He stood, shooting his cuffs and straightening his tie. "I'm sorry. But I'm done being your once-a-year fuck boy."

I watched him turn away from me, knowing full well that I might be tossing my last shot at real happiness straight out the window by letting him go. Then I let him go without a kiss or a hug or anything acknowledging the intense years between us. I picked up the ring once the elevator doors had snicked shut behind him. I even slipped it onto my finger, impressed by its heft. I left it on as I took a shower, got dressed and finished packing, my eyes dry but my chest aching with anticipated loss.

I rode the elevator down, the ring still on my finger. Before walking out to the waiting limo, I stepped up to the concierge and asked to speak with Mike. Once I was in the general management suite of offices, I saw him, standing in the hall, talking with a woman who smiled up at him in a way that did not send a jolt of jealousy through me like it might have even a year ago.

He spotted me. His face brightened, and he rushed over, pulling me into his office, gathering me close. I buried my nose in his starchy, cotton-covered chest. Then I slid the ring off my finger, pressed it into his palm, closed his fingers around it and kissed his knuckles.

"Thank you," I said. I was about to say something asinine like "you'll always be special to me" but that had a ring of fakery to it even I couldn't bear. He would be. But he knew that.

"Miranda," he said. I put my finger to his lips and shook my head. "Listen," he mumbled.

"Shh. No more. Go and live your life, okay? And I'll do the same." I opened the door and ducked out, hurrying down the hall, pretending no one was watching me break up with the rich, gorgeous, now very sad boss. I slid into the backseat of the limo and stared straight ahead until the last minute. When I turned and looked out the back window, Mike was there, one hand lifted. I sucked in a breath, turned on my phone and prepared to send a text to Sawyer, asking for a real date.

I'd left it off for that last twelve hours, wanting nothing to interrupt my last experience with Mike. As soon as the thing came to life, my screen filled with messages, each more desperate than the last, from my assistant, and Ashley, and one from Sawyer himself that took my breath away:

I need you. Please come home.

Chapter Fourteen

I tried to respond to them all, but the cell network was jammed and nothing would go through. Cursing when the telltale beeps of a dropped call hit my ear over and over again, I paced around, attempting to locate a decent signal. Something had happened to the main cell tower, a blown transformer or some shit, so everyone was doing the same communication-seeking dance around the airport.

I gave up after a while and got coffee while I waited for my plane. But the caffeine hit my stomach funny, so I threw half of it away, hearing Sawyer fussing in absentia at the wastefulness of it. Right as they were announcing first class boarding for my flight to Detroit, a call came through from Ashley.

"Hello? Ashley? What the hell is going on?"

"Oh god, Miranda, it's awful. It's Emma."

It took me a few seconds to figure out whom she meant. "Sawyer's daughter? What happened?"

"He didn't show up for the inspection of his new house, so your assistant called me."

I tried to motion for the lady waiting by the jet way to hang on a sec, heart in my throat.

"It was a car accident. A bunch of girls. One of them is dead. Emma's in the hospital, in a coma or something," Ashley said.

"Holy shit."

"I've been sitting with him," she said, making the green monster rear its ugly and badly timed head. "Poor thing," she said in a tone I didn't recognize or like very much. "He wanted me to stay. So I did." She sighed. I hung up, unwilling to hear another word and knowing I could tell her later the signal cut us off.

I hurried on board, seething, frantic for Sawyer and with a sick feeling churning around in my stomach. The flight seemed to take days.

Once we landed, I grabbed my bag and hustled out to find a ride. When I was settled in the back of one, I called Sawyer.

"Hello," he said, his voice croaky and strange. "Miranda?"

"Yes, yes, it's me. What... where...."

"U of M hospital," he said, giving me a room number. "Hurry. Please."

I told the driver and gnawed on my fingernail the entire trip, willing the man to go faster. Mike sent me a text. I deleted it without answering. My assistant sent me several messages that I answered quickly, telling her where I'd be in case she needed me. I jumped out at the hospital entrance and rolled my suitcase behind me, seeking someone to point me in the right direction.

Emma was on the fifth floor, in an intensive care room. The nurse was at first reluctant to let me in, but I shot her an evil eye and she backed off. Muscling past my innate fear of hospitals, I pushed open the door, keeping my eyes averted from the figure in the bed hooked up to a million tubes. Focusing instead on the man in the chair next to it. He had his hands pressed together, fingers white knuckled. His forehead was on them. His lips were moving. I hesitated, unwilling to interrupt.

As if sensing me, he looked up, his blue eyes haunted, his hair a mess. I swallowed. He rose to his feet slowly, as if it hurt him. The band that had tightened around my chest the minute Mike had pressed the marriage thing on me loosened. I went to him. He grabbed onto me and held me close, pressing his face into my shoulder. We stood like this for what felt like a long time.

"Sawyer," I whispered, running my fingers through his tangled hair. "You need to eat. The nurse said..."

"Sh," he said, drawing away from me, his expression furious. "Don't you start on me, too. I'm not leaving her."

"All right," I said as he dropped back into his seat. I put my hands on his shoulders. "What happened?"

"Fucking god damned teenagers," he muttered, shocking me with the profanity. "Mother fucking phones and texts and... fuck." He leapt up and started pacing around the small room, dragging fingers through his hair. "My fault," he muttered, staring down at his long fingers before curling them into fists. "My fault," he said again.

"Stop that," I said, putting my arms around his waist, surprising myself with how natural it felt to do that. "It's not and you know it."

He sighed and looked up at the ceiling, then down at me. "It was the middle of the day," he said, his voice hoarse again. "Perfect weather. Bunch of girls in the car. She was in the passenger's seat, buckled in. The girl driving was changing the song on her phone. The other girls were joking around, not paying attention. She drifted into the path of a god damned giant truck."

A loud cacophony of alarms went off, making us jump away from each other. Nurses rushed in. Doctors followed. Sawyer clung to me as we watched them revive the girl on the bed with electric shocks. Every time they applied it, Sawyer groaned more audibly. Finally, her heart decided to keep beating. The medical staff backed away.

"Mr. Callahan," one of the scrub-clad doctors said. "I'm sorry. But this only makes me more certain. You are going to have to make a decision." He checked his tablet computer. "In the next twelve hours. Like I told you earlier."

Sawyer made a strange growling sound low in his throat, then let go of me and lunged for the man in scrubs, nearly wrestling him to the ground before the nurses and I were able to drag him off.

He stayed on the floor, staring down at the tiles. I crouched beside him, patting his shoulder, unsure what in the world I could do. The bleeps from Emma's heartbeat filled the room.

Finally, the door opened again and Ashley walked in carrying coffees and her phone. She frowned when she didn't see us at first, then set her stuff on a table, and reached down to touch Sawyer's arm. We knelt on either side of him, as he seemed frozen, unwilling or unable to move. Our eyes met. Hers narrowed ever so slightly.

"Sawyer, honey, let's get you up. I brought the coffee." He turned his head towards her, blinking fast, as if just waking up from a long sleep. "That's right. I'm back." She shot me an odd look. "Miranda's here too. Let us help you up off the floor, okay?"

He nodded. His eyes met mine, pleading with me to fix it, to turn back the clock, to take away this moment. I held out my hand. He put his in it, and Ashley and I dragged him up and back to his chair. He resumed his position, praying, I assumed, over what was left of his daughter.

Chapter Fifteen

S awyer
Four Days Earlier

"Ashley," Sawyer said, clearing his throat when it didn't want to cooperate at first. "Hi. It's Sawyer."

"Hey Sawyer. How're things?" She kept her voice neutral, to her credit.

"Fine, fine. Listen, um, wondering if you'd like to go out again sometime." He winced at himself.

"Sure," she said. "When?"

Actually, I'd like for you to come over now, get naked and jump into bed with me. It will really go a long way towards dispelling all these images I have of your friend, Miranda, my red-headed fantasy object, getting her brains banged out by her Vegas boyfriend. You're my only hope, since you're as close as I've gotten to a woman's body in a damn long time, and I am one hard up dude. How does that sound?

"Tonight? Maybe? Do you like sushi? I know this great place over in Ypsi—"

"Sure, but I'm not a big sushi fan, sorry. I worry about the mercury, you know? How about I cook? Do you like Italian?"

"Love it," knowing this for a ploy to get him in her house and not caring as long as he could get laid and shove Miranda out of his head. "What time?"

They firmed up the details. He said he'd bring the wine. After he hung up, he put his head on his arms on the table, sighing with relief.

"Hey daddy-o," Emma said, as she drifted into the kitchen. "It's leftovers night. I have some of that white chili."

"I'm going out," he said, his voice tight. "Uh, sort of a date."

"Oh, cool," she said, staring into the depths of the fridge. "Staying over? Is it Miranda?" She raised her eyebrows at him. He frowned.

"No, and no." He got up and poured a glass of water, sensing her gaze on him. "Okay, maybe a sleep over. But no, it's not Miranda." He turned to face her.

"Oh, damn," she said, pouting. "But awesome-sauce on the maybe sleep over." She kissed his scruffy cheek. "Might wanna do a little man-scaping on this," she said, tugging on his facial hair. "Chicks typically aren't into rug burn."

"Will you please not talk like that?"

She giggled and pinched his cheek. His racing pulse calmed as he glanced down at his phone for the millionth time, wishing to see a message from Miranda. Why he'd put her off at her place when they'd been so close to something amazing, he had no clue. He was waiting for the committee to show up any minute now and revoke his man card. Willing, eager, half naked woman: check. Rock solid erection: check. What was his major malfunction?

Man card pulling was a definite. And that nosy parker question about her pregnancy? Jesus, what had gotten into him? But the words had leapt out of his mouth without checking in with his brain and ruined everything.

It was why he'd reached out to Ashley. He had to prove to himself he could do this. "This" of course being something he'd once been able to pull off without a ton of effort. Women loved a good-looking cop. One woman in particular, he recalled, a cute, petite bartender chick, who taught English Lit part time at a small college. He'd been the first on the scene when she'd been in a scary accident, some guy rear ending her on the interstate, mashing her piece of shit car between his and the one in front of her, nearly folding it into an accordion.

It had been a huge mess of a thing, in spaghetti junction at rush hour in Louisville. It took three hours to clear it all up. Afterward, he'd rushed to the hospital to check on her, the pretty girl with the likely concussion and broken ribs who'd been sitting on the side of the interstate, dazed and about to walk straight into traffic when he'd arrived. She'd been all right, admitted a few days for observation. He'd brought her flowers, then a fast-food hamburger when she'd asked for it. Smitten, over the moon, twitter-pated, he'd been, as his mother liked to remind him.

But she was a tiger once they'd finagled a way to hook up, the first time after hours in the back of the deserted restaurant where she worked. He had two roommates. Couldn't afford to live on his own yet. She lived in her parent's basement. They spent hours, naked, lolling around on his bed in his tiny room in the smelly, generic apartment, watching movies and eating cheap pizza while his roommates came and went.

He'd not really given a ton of thought to birth control once they'd established that neither of them had any nasty diseases to share. She claimed to be on top of that, so he'd left the rubbers in the drawer with glee. Three months into their relationship, she got word that her resume had been moved up the line and she was being considered for a real teaching job at a real university in Michigan. Not just any university either. The big dog. The one in Ann Arbor. Sawyer had been so sex addled at that point it barely registered.

The morning she woke him, crying on her side of his frameless mattress in the empty room that smelled like sex and insecticide, something shifted in his universe. "I'm pregnant," she said. "I need four hundred dollars so I can take care of it."

"Take care of it," he'd repeated, struggling to sit and wake fully. "What are you talking about?"

"An abortion, Sawyer," she said, sticking her legs into her jeans and dragging one of his sweatshirts down over her bare torso. "Do you have four hundred bucks, or what?"

He did. But he convinced her they could make a go of it, raise a child together. They got married at the courthouse with his colleagues for witnesses and threw a little party for themselves before breaking the news to their parents. Sawyer was thirty-three years old and had saved nearly twenty thousand dollars, living small and cheap for the past few years. Helen was twenty-seven. The day of her first ultrasound, she got the word. The University of Michigan wanted her to teach for them, first as adjunct, with the very real possibility of full-time professorship around the corner.

They moved. Sawyer got a desk job at the Ann Arbor police department. He was loath to dip into his savings but they did to buy a house in Burns Park a year after Emma was born and Helen got her first bump to professor full time with benefits. Sawyer adored his daughter and spent the bulk of his time with the girl, carting her around to hardware stores and installing her in her playpen while he tinkered with the 1940's bungalow on Olivia Avenue. When the girl started school, he got his own part time professorial job, teaching accounting at night. He'd gotten his degree in it years ago but never used it other than to manage his own household with a strict adherence to his spreadsheeted budget.

The years past in a proverbial blur. And one day, Neil Jensen, his buddy with the handy man outfit, told him he'd make a great real estate appraiser. He was practical and level headed and there were too damn many appraisers messing up the market with over valuations. So he got that license easily and began earning twice his teaching salary as the appraiser the realtors loved to hate, while hanging onto his part time desk job at the police department and teaching accounting a few nights a month.

It was about that time he noticed something was wrong with his wife. She had night sweats and headaches and would flip moods so quickly he felt like he lived in a non-stop PMS universe.

He insisted she see a doctor. She put him off. She claimed he was stifling her with his overbearing hyper organization. He told her she was lazy, couldn't get her head out of the clouds long enough to figure out how to balance a checkbook. They stopped having sex, which for them was a Big Deal. She moved into the second bedroom, claiming she needed to be up late to work on her novel.

When the University Press published her novel, he skipped her launch party after one of their biggest fights yet the night before. He was so horny he ached deep in his bones, but he would be damned if he'd give her any part of him just then. Something was wrong with her. Sawyer was self-aware enough to admit that he never should have married her. She was too flighty and self-absorbed.

But he'd look at his pretty daughter, all done up in her pink bows and her girlie outfits. He'd kiss her and put her to bed and remind himself it had been for her, for Emma. And it had been the right thing.

He closed his eyes, reliving the moment he'd fired up Helen's laptop after she'd finally succumbed to the fast-moving cancer, after hours spent arguing with her, giving in to her strange requests as she got sicker and sicker, then holding her in his arms as she slipped away.

"Yo, Dad," Emma yelped, interrupting his unpleasant trip down Helen memory lane. "I need twenty bucks."

"What for?" he asked, reaching for his wallet. "You don't need gas money. I still possess your car keys."

"It's a just-in-case," she said, taking the money. "If you have a sleepover tonight. I'm getting lunch with Jackie and her sister tomorrow. She's driving. It's a teacher's in-service day. No school."

He sighed, exhausted beyond his years. "House is sold," he said, smiling when she refilled his glass of water. "With a back up offer in placc."

"Nice. Miranda does a good job, eh?" She winked at him. Sawyer winced, recalling just how good a job she did and what a jerk he'd been to her. He didn't even really know why he'd acted that way, other than the fact of her leaving, heading out to meet that man, the Vegas man. The guy, not him, who still had his man-card. He groaned a little under his breath. "What's wrong Daddy-o? Need to talk about it?"

He smiled at her in spite of his aggravation. "Nah, it's grown up stuff kiddo." He patted her cheek. "Homework done?"

"Nope, not yet."

"Best get on it, then."

"Yessir," she said, saluting him. He blew out a breath, relieved that she was in a good mood for a change.

Chapter Sixteen

S awyer glared at himself in the mirror. He'd gotten used to his beard and didn't want to get rid of it, but he'd be damned if it kept him from getting laid at this juncture. So he located the electric shaver, but when he pulled it out of its storage case, it was so clogged he couldn't get it to turn on.

"Emma Callahan, get your tail in here right now," he yelled.

"What?" she said, slouching around the corner into the bathroom. "I'm busy." She held up her calculus book as if he needed proof.

"Why are you using my razor?" He held it up, meeting her math book and raising the stakes with a lot of pubic hair. "For your...your..." He waved a hand in the general direction he meant.

"Because, Padre, you won't let me wax it, remember?"

His face got hot. "Yes, I remember that, but I figured you'd use shave cream and a regular razor. This thing is expensive and you've been using it and not cleaning it out before you put it away. Now it's clogged and won't work."

She slumped in the doorway, picking at her black painted fingernails. "Whatever," she said. The one word he could live his entire lifetime and never hear again with glee.

He sensed the rage crawling up his spine, ready to explode in his head. He clenched his jaw, knowing this for a dumb, unwinnable, and therefore unnecessary fight. But he was stressed out, worried about Miranda, worried about himself. He didn't really want to go to Ashley's house, even if it meant he'd end his self-imposed dry spell.

"Fuck!" He spit out. Emma flinched at the unfamiliar curse word. He threw the razor into the sink. It broke into six or seven pieces. After glaring up at himself for a few more minutes, he grabbed the scissors, shave cream and a fresh pack of razor blades. "Beat it," he said to his daughter's reflection over his shoulder. "I am not in the mood."

Thirty minutes later, the deed was done, at least as close as he was willing to get with it. Realizing he'd be late if he didn't get a move on, he grabbed a shower and took a while picking out his clothes before cursing again under his breath and choosing things he didn't even pay attention to. He was gonna be out of them for most of this date anyway, he reasoned. If all went to plan.

He pounded down the steps in his sock feet, ignoring Emma, who was sitting at the kitchen table, earphones over her ears, whittling away at her calc. The girl was a straight-A student,with high SAT scores. She wanted to go to an Ivy League school and Sawyer could afford it thanks to his well-documented and much-maligned miserly ways. It was all good. He took a long breath, then touched her shoulder. She flinched and glared up at him, not taking the headphones off.

"I'm sorry," he mouthed.

"Whatever," she mouthed back, looking away from him. He waited a few seconds. "Nice face," she said, overly loud.

He gave her a thumbs up, tucking a Viagra tablet into his pocket for good measure. His doctor had prescribed them at his last check-up a few months ago and the damn things had been sitting in the cabinet, unused since then. Not that he'd had any trouble getting it up around Miranda, he mused as he grabbed his keys and headed for the door.

"Dad, wait," Emma said, stopping him in his tracks. He turned. A strip of condoms hit him in the chest and then dropped to the floor. He glared down at them, then up at his seventeen-going-on-thirty daughter. She parroted his thumbs up. He snatched the damn things and gave the door a good hard slam on his way out.

On the drive over, his thoughts wandered to the sultry redhead he'd wanted since the first time he'd laid eyes on her. He'd only had that feeling once before. It was probably why he kept putting Miranda off, poor woman. He didn't want to subject her to his baggage. The way he hung onto the giant mistake that had been his marriage could be a real buzz kill, he knew.

Miranda was probably having an orgasm right at this moment with the gigolo. He winced when his body responded without the chemical assistance of the pill still in his pocket.

"No, no, no," he said to himself, doing a quick mental breakdown of his retirement fund, his investments, his life's balance sheet to ward off a premature woody. He pulled into Ashley's drive and sat a few minutes gripping the steering wheel and forcing himself to remember why he'd initiated this encounter in the first place. He took two of the condoms off the strip, stuck them in his wallet, got out, and put his wallet in his back pocket. He could smell the rich cheese and tomato sauce already. His stomach grumbled.

He knocked on her door. She answered it, wearing nothing but a smile. He blinked. She pulled him inside, shut the door, and jumped into his arms. Dazed, and with a boner that drained every ounce of blood out of his body, he kissed her, tromping around and trying to find a horizontal surface. He settled for dropping her onto the couch, crouching between her legs and bringing her to a screaming orgasm with his lips, tongue and fingers, all the while thinking "Miranda, Miranda, Miranda," in his head.

He came up for air, groping for his belt, his zipper, anything to ease the pressure that had built behind it, his vision going a little wonky around the edges. She pushed him back, so he flopped onto the sisal rug-covered floor with an awkward thunk, tugging his jeans down and off. Already feeling the rug burn on his ass, he yanked her forward. "Condom," he ground out. "In my wallet."

As he lay there trying hard not to pass out, she got it, rolled it down over him, then lowered herself onto his straining dick. He grabbed her thighs, closed his eyes and started counting backward from a thousand, knowing if he did anything but that he'd come in about three seconds. She tightened around him, rolling her hips, bouncing so her tits jounced up and down in front of his bleary eyes. "Oh baby," she groaned when he was able to release his death grip on one of her thighs and grab a boob.

That did it. He came with a loud, embarrassing moan and shudder, worried when the room went black for a few seconds before her pretty face came into focus again.

She kissed him softly, her tongue exploring as she rolled around on him, obviously seeking a second orgasm. He was a giver, so he obliged, sucking on her nipple as she rubbed against him and then came with a quick cry of pleasure, tightening around his still hard cock, making him grunt.

"Welcome to my house, Sawyer," she said, breathless, flushed, and lovely. She rose to her feet, leaving him loose-limbed, and limp, but for his dick which still filled out the condom. He wanted to sleep. But she was standing over him, holding out her hand.

He got up, tugged the condom off and put it in the paper towel she handed him. He grabbed his jeans, found the bathroom and stood, hanging on to the edge of her sink for a few minutes.

"Dinner," Ashley called out.

"Be there in a minute," he said, staring at himself, noting the strange, baby-ish feel of his own facial skin, re-exposed and for the good, he guessed, since he'd gone right for oral.

It would be beyond rude to skip out now, even though his brain was screaming at him to do exactly that. It would shame his upbringing. No son of Eileen Callahan would act in such a way, and he knew it. So he smiled at the redressed version of Ashley—oh crap, what was her last name? He uncorked the wine he'd left at the front door, poured them each a glass, then sat at the table where she indicated he should.

He sipped the wine, grateful for the alcohol as it dulled the bizarre sharpness that hovered around his edges, reminding him he had just used the lovely woman humming in the kitchen for nothing but sex. The lasagna was perfection. The bread crisp and buttery. The salad astringent and a great complement to the rest of the meal. They talked, to his surprise, mostly about Miranda.

"I think she's amazing," Ashley said at one point.

"Yeah," he said, trying to force another bite of food into his mouth. "Me too."

He held up his wine glass by way of interrupting her monologue about the woman he'd pictured when he'd climaxed on the floor a few minutes ago. "You're a great cook." She blushed. Charming, he thought, sipping and studying her. Gorgeous, too.

No, Callahan. No more wives.

He shook his head.

"You all right?" She stood up to clear his place. He started to reach for her arm so he could tug her into his lap, already comparing her slightness to the solid, sexy curves he'd had in his hands, albeit briefly, the other day. Right before he turned into a weak sister and shoved Miranda onto the plane, destined for her week of perfect sex with a guy not himself.

But he stopped himself. "I'm fine." He stared down at his plate, which had become empty without him recalling much about eating the food on it.

She cleared the table in silence, leaving him to finish his wine. By the time she returned, he knew what he had to do. He rose, pulled her into his arms, kissed her forehead, and said, "I have to go now."

"I think you should stay," she said, as she unbuckled his belt.

Sawyer woke with a grunt. He sat, trying to figure out where he was for a few seconds before he recalled. He was with Ashley. She of the unknown last name and the kick ass blowjob skills. He flopped back onto her frilly pillow case, breath rasping his throat as the dream memories faded, and reality of what he'd done came back to him piecemeal, reminding him of all the nights he'd spent staring at the ceiling of the guest room of his own house.

He slid out from under Ashley's draped over arm and leg and found the bathroom, emptying his bladder before creeping down the short hall to the kitchen for some water. He drank it, reveling in the sated feeling from a couple of great orgasms after years-long drought. Funny, considering he'd been such a pussy magnet for so many years before Helen. He wished he could go home now, but knew that was uncool in the current situation, so he headed for the bedroom. A buzzing phone waylaid him. He fished around in his jeans pocket for it, worried, realizing he'd not checked in with Emma for several hours.

The message was from her. Daddy-o hope U R having a great time with your new lady friend. I'm going to bed now. I'll see you tmrw. (heart shape)

He sighed, wondering if she was lying through her teenaged lying teeth and was not at home right now, taking full advantage of his absence. Sleepiness stole over him, replacing the guilt at not being home for her, and for fucking Ashley's ever-loving brains out after she'd sucked him so hard he'd yelled with pleasure, all the while picturing a completely different woman. It was probably why the sex dreams were back. That had been one long guilty pleasure, he knew. And something Helen had manipulated at the end of her life, knowing her own culpability.

He slid back under the cover, curving his body around Ashley's, draping his arm over her bony hip. Sleep descended fast. So did the dreams.

Chapter Seventeen

Miranda

I had the staff bring in a recliner for Sawyer after a while, so he could maybe catch a nap. But he balked, unwilling to move from Emma's bedside. I sat in it instead, feeling myself drop off, desperate for a few winks, not even sure what time, or even what day it was.

I opened my eyes at one point and found the room filled with people in cop uniforms. They occupied every nook and cranny of the space, hiding Sawyer from my view. Their voices were low, murmuring, unremarkable. I let my eyes drift shut again.

When I opened them again, the room was full of sobbing teenagers. Girls and boys alike were ringed around Emma's bed, some silent, some crying. Sawyer had not moved. He had his forehead on his clenched fists still. I got up, feeling stiff and weird. I wandered out to the hall, glad I had my suitcase since that meant I had my toothbrush. I located a bathroom and emerged feeling somewhat better, or at least not with dragon breath.

A young guy I finally figured out was Neil Jensen, he of the HandyMan Inc. and the save-the-lost-teenagers life goals, was kneeling next to Sawyer. He glanced up when I entered the room, then turned back to keep up the vigil with his friend. Still unwilling to look at the poor girl on the bed, I slipped back out into the hall.

A tall woman was standing outside Emma's room, talking on the phone. Her remarkable resemblance to Sawyer warranted a double take. Ashley walked up, holding more coffee, her eyes red-rimmed and bloodshot. She put an arm around the woman's shoulders. The woman ended her call and sobbed into my friend's neck. I waited, an outsider looking in.

"They've located recipients," the Sawyer look-alike woman said, standing back from Ashley and wiping her streaming eyes. "Corneas, lungs, liver, kidneys, skin. Oh my dear god," she said, sucking in a huge breath and looking up at the ceiling. "I can't do this."

Ashley seemed at a loss. She glanced over at me. I walked closer. "Hi," I said, putting a hand on the sobbing woman's arm. "I'm Miranda."

The woman glanced up and met my eyes. "I'm Laura. Sawyer's sister."

A loud roar of anger made us all flinch, then rush to Emma's room. Sawyer was backed against a wall, staring at the man in a suit, clipboard in hand, bracketed by a priest and some other religious type, I guessed, by the look of her. Probably some Unitarian, so as not to offend anyone with overt religiosity.

They had Sawyer cornered, I realized, just as Laura ran to him and gripped him close. The two of them held onto each other. Tears slid down my face and I held onto Ashley, no longer caring who was sleeping with whom. All the while, Neil remained on his knees by Emma's bed.

After a few minutes, or maybe a few hours, I no longer had a frame of reference for time passing. Sawyer and Laura stood, forehead-to-forehead, talking. Then they turned to the man with the clipboard. Sawyer took it, signed some papers and handed them over. Laura took both his hands, and they turned to the bed. Neil rose and put an arm around his shoulders. Ashley sucked in a breath. I held onto her, not letting her run out of the room. "He needs us all right now. Don't flake," I hissed under my breath. But I would have given just about anything not to witness the next hour in that room. Anything.

· · · ·

I STUMBLED THROUGH the next day or two, not ever talking with Sawyer even though I spent plenty of time in his house, handling the many visitors and donations of food. He kept to himself, only communicating with his sister or Neil. Laura was an amazing, self-contained bundle of energy, determined to get past this, to help her brother. But I caught her more than once crumpled into a corner of a couch or sitting in a chair, staring into space.

Somehow, the few days I'd been in Nevada rejecting Mike's proposal in hopes of finding myself in Sawyer's world, the entire universe had tilted on its axis, upending all plans, be they carefully made or otherwise.

I had a fair bit of work to do, placating the buyer of his house and the seller of the house he was to buy, showing them news reports of the crash and begging everyone's forgiveness for an unanticipated delay of the proceedings. None of which anyone could predict.

Luckily, everyone understood. The poor man, a widow already, had come within hours of turning off his only daughter's life support. But she'd blinked open her eyes, stared straight up at him and said, "Daddy? Where am I? What happened?"

Who could argue with his need for time to process all of that? Not to mention Emma's anticipated long recovery.

The first night home after Emma's body had almost been harvested for her organs, Laura had called me, frantic, not knowing where else to turn since neither Neil nor Ashley had been unable to calm Sawyer down.

I raced to his house, heart pounding, dressed in grungy jeans and turtleneck. After screeching into the driveway, I jumped out and tackled him as he was about to take another swing at my damn sign with a sledgehammer. He was drunk. That much I knew from Laura's intel. So I knocked him off balance enough to send the sledge flying off into the dark front yard. He lay on his back, breath rasping in his throat, staring over my shoulder as I pinned his arms to the ground.

"Cut the shit, Callahan," I said, as calmly as I could. He met my gaze, the streetlight casting shadows into the hollows of his cheeks. "Destroying my sign will not solve anything."

He stopped breathing long enough to worry me. Then he blew out a boozy breath, rolling us so he had me pinned beneath him. I let him. "Why did you leave?" he demanded. Before I could respond, he jumped up and ran for his front door. I lay there for a few minutes, listening to him bellowing and slamming things around inside his house.

When I sat up, staring into the gloom, I felt his hurt deep in my gut. But I wanted nothing more than to get in my car and bolt. That selfish thought got me moving again.

I stood and headed towards the house. Every light seemed to be on, illuminating the yard in all directions. As I trudged up the steps to the front porch, Ashley appeared in the doorway. "I'm glad you're here," she said.

The sight of her wringing her fingers, her red-rimmed eyes, her very presence in this house made my ears buzz with the sort of jealousy that was all the more ridiculous for its inappropriateness. Walking past her, I noted clothes, mail, and other crap scattered around, which ramped up my anxiety about the man's state of mind. Laura was in the kitchen, standing at the sink, her hands buried in a mound of soap bubbles. I flopped into a chair. The table was covered in hospital paperwork, and, I noted, the two contracts we had. One on this house and on the new one. With a sigh, I tugged them to me for something to look at that was not related to the near death of a promising young woman.

"I wrestled him into bed," Neil said, coming into the room. "God damn me, what a cluster fuck this is."

"But she's really okay, right?" I asked, my voice hoarse.

"She seems to be fine, other than the fact that she's paralyzed from the waist down. But the docs think that will resolve in another twelve hours."

"Then why did he lose it?"

Neil drained the beer he'd left on the table and sighed. "He blames himself. It's his core failing."

A silence fell. Ashley joined us, took a bottle of vodka from the freezer, and poured four shots. I stared at mine a minute before tossing it back. My mind wandered to the calendar. The time had come for my life to change. I was about to undergo a long-planned three-sixty into a much different world. I sighed, wondering why I never told Sawyer about it, since I'd told him everything else. That might have changed things between us, kept me home from Vegas.

Story of my life, I thought as I stared at Ashley and processed that she was here in my place and planned to stay that way.

I got up, hugged each of them, and offered to tidy up before I left.

"He keeps asking me if you're still here," Laura whispered in my ear. I blinked, processing this, recalling how comfortable Ashley was in Sawyer's about-to-be-sold house.

"Sawyer and I... we just have some business transactions together."

"Really," she said, leaning back and crossing her arms, giving me the look I'd come to know as the patented Callahan-BS detector.

"Really. And speaking of, I'm going to need to know if he's able to go through with them both. I have sympathetic buyers on this end and a seller on the other, but need to update them pretty soon as to our adjusted schedule."

"I'm not backing out." This from a low, scratchy voice, making me turn and see Sawyer at the foot of the stairs. "Don't worry. You'll get paid."

"Dude, I told you to stay put," Neil said, not getting up as if realizing the futility of standing in his friend's way.

He stomped past us. Laura frowned at his retreating back.

"Give me and Emma a three week extension," he said before pouring himself a giant splash of whisky. "We'll make it happen."

Laura followed me to my car. The distinct snap of oncoming fall was in the air tonight and I welcomed it like I never had before. I gripped the steering wheel. This was my life. I'd set it up this way almost six years ago and was not about to let anyone else in, not now. It was time for things to change.

"How long can you stick around?" I asked Laura as she leaned into my car window.

"Another week, maybe two," she said. "But I'll figure something out if he and Emma need me to stay longer."

"Call me if you need anything. But he's in good hands with you and Ashley." I knew that was what my friend wanted now. And she rarely didn't get what she wanted.

Laura patted my arm, stood and walked back to the house without contradicting me like I wanted her to. On my way back to my condo, I hit a quick dial number on my phone. "Mom," I said, when she answered, trying to keep the quaver out of my voice. "Can you bring him early? This week? I bought a house and I want him to see it. I want you to see it." My voice broke, and I had to pull over when tears clouded my eyes.

"Sure hon," she said, chipper and bright and organized and all the things I wanted to be once upon a time. "Want to talk to him?"

"Sure," I said, swiping my eyes. "Please, yes."

"Hi, Mommy," my son said, his sweet voice filling the car and making me burst into tears all over again.

Chapter Eighteen

S awyer
   October

"Where do you want this?" Ashley asked, jolting him out of a semi-stupor. "Honey?"

Sawyer blinked fast, trying to figure out who was calling him that, and why. He kept losing track of time. A few hours every day would fly by and he'd find himself staring out a window, surprised by the looming darkness. Understandable, said the shrink he'd been assigned until he'd gotten the woman's first bill and subsequently cancelled the rest of their sessions. He didn't need to pay someone to listen to him bemoan his terrible life. He just needed to move forward. Forward motion was all he had left to him now. Forward motion was what he kept telling Emma to use as she regained feeling and movement in her hips and legs.

He watched Ashley move around his new space, setting down potted plants, or putting away towels. She'd hardly left his side for the past six weeks. Or his bed. Also good, since his long-neglected libido had roared back to life, giving him a reason to get up in the morning. Mainly, it seemed, so he could have sex with her in every room of his old house, then in every corner of this one while Emma languished in the hospital.

Using his extra emotional energy on screwing instead of hating himself had been his solution. Right after Miranda had tackled him in front of his house. He had hoped she'd stay, but she hadn't. Ashley had. Ashley had what he needed and willingly gave it to him.

"I need to get to my office," she said, pulling her long blond hair back and giving him an instant hard on. God, he was craven, he thought, as he moved swiftly to her, kissing her so he wouldn't have to talk to her. She only protested for a half second as he picked her up, pulling her legs around his waist and stumbling into the first-floor bedroom.

Later, he lay staring up at the ceiling while she showered, re-dressed, kissed his sweaty bare chest, and left. Tears burned his eyes, so he lurched up, got his own shower, and started unpacking, cranking bad eighties yacht rock music up high to drown out the sound of his own voice, berating himself for not being a better father. He found himself sitting on the wonky front porch a few hours later, holding an untouched beer and staring into the dusk, wondering how and when he'd gotten there. It was chilly, fully launched into fall now. He squeezed his eyes shut, dumped the brew onto the grass and went inside. There was work to be done. Emma had been discharged and would be home within a couple of hours.

He finished setting up her portable bed in the downstairs bedroom. It was a temporary situation, they'd both agreed, but a necessary one while she did daily physical therapy to help her do things like walk. Ashley had bought some girly crap for the room that he stared at a solid thirty minutes before abandoning all of it. Emma had her own decorating ideas, and he'd let her decide about that.

Once the room was ready, he still had another hour before the ambulance would arrive. Laura and Neil were coming in it with Emma so he could finish the house stuff. He pulled out his laptop and dropped into some appraisal work. The community college had given him the semester off, to his dismay. He didn't need the money, but required the distraction. So he'd doubled his appraisal load and welcomed the familiar rush of complaints from realtors and lenders alike. Neil had a fresh crop of employees and Sawyer relished the time he spent raking massive lawns, blowing out miles of sprinklers, hauling piles of junk and playing bad cop to some of the harder cases.

He stared down at his phone, not realizing he'd picked it up, and then answered a string of text messages from Jack, reassuring him that all was well, Emma was fine and coming home today. He ignored his old friend's questions about Miranda. It had gotten way too complicated to explain.

Then he called her.

"Hi, Sawyer," Miranda said, her voice neutral and business-like. He smiled, his chest loosening at the sound of her voice. "What can I do for you?"

"Oh, nothing," he said, fiddling with his fountain pen on the desk. "I heard you moved."

"Yes," she said.

The silence went beyond awkward, but he had no frame of reference for his need to listen to her talk. "So, why'd you do that? I liked your condo."

"Well, let's see, that would remain not your business."

"Sorry," he said, genuinely hurt. People cut him so much slack lately. Her bluntness sliced through the fog he kept close around him in a surprisingly pleasant change of pace. "You're right."

"What do you want, Sawyer? I'm sort of busy. I figured you had your hands full. Doesn't Emma get home today?"

He propped his bare feet up on the desk. "I miss you."

She didn't speak for a few beats. "You miss me," she repeated. "Funny, I couldn't tell, given how you've gotten in so deep with my friend." She emphasized the last word, then sighed. "Listen, Sawyer, I'm not trying to be bitchy. I know you've been through a lot. I'm happy for you, and for her, for you both and for Emma. Now, if you'll excuse me..."

"I'd like to see your place," he blurted out, surprising himself.

"Maybe someday," she said.

"I still consider you my friend. All that stuff you told me about your ex and your last few years of debauchery. I know it was hard to open up like that."

"I can tell you've been to a shrink," she said.

"Yeah, a few times. But it was—"

"Let me guess. A waste of money."

He chuckled. "Yeah, that."

Rain pattered against the window. He watched it a while, letting their silence stretch a bit longer than was polite. "Anyway," she said. "Gotta go. Give my best to Emma."

"All right," he said. "Bye." He ended the call just as the ambulance pulled into the driveway, ready to discharge his alive but wounded daughter into her new life.

Rain pounded on the roof as he lay awake. Ashley was curled into his side. He kissed her hair, then slid out of bed. He was pleasantly sore in places he'd forgotten were pleasant when sore. His mind was blank. The house's dark silence echoed with memories of his previous life. He stood in the kitchen, watching the impressive non-stop downpour for a few minutes.

Emma had been her old self for the most part, bitching about the ugly view out of her downstairs bedroom window and griping that the internet wasn't fast enough to stream Netflix. All of which had almost reduced him to tears. He was blind with gratitude that he'd made the medical team give him another fifteen minutes with her before they turned off her life support. But almost as equally furious that they'd missed the fact that she was not, in fact, brain dead. And the low buzz of rage at himself for letting her get into this situation never quite faded.

A noise hit his ears, confusing him until he recognized it as his phone. It was vibrating its way across the desk in the small office alcove at the other end of the kitchen. He grabbed it, heart pounding when he saw the name.

"What's wrong?" he barked into it, running his hand across his beard.

"Oh shit, I'm sorry," Miranda said. There was a loud sound in the background, as if she were standing outside in the rain. "I'm sorry. Can you help? The god damned downspout busted and water is pouring into my basement and... now I think the sewer line's backing up."

"Address?"

She gave it to him. It was a street over on the city's west side, near a popular elementary school. He said he'd be right there.

"What's going on," Ashley mumbled, rolling over to look at him as he pulled a sweatshirt over his head.

"Miranda's got a flooded basement," he said, feeling more energized than he had in weeks.

"I'll come too." She swung her legs to the side of the bed.

"No, no, it's fine." He kissed her forehead. "I've got it. Stay here with Emma for me."

He peeked in on her before he headed into the garage to grab his tools. "Hey," he said, coming to her bedside to kiss her cheek.

"What time is it? Ugh. Do I have to get up?"

"No, baby. I'm just going to help Miranda with something at her new house."

Emma blinked up at him. "Miranda, eh? I thought Ashley was going for step-monster status."

He shrugged. His daughter, ever the radar for his low-lying emotions, frowned at him. "Dad, you need to..."

He patted her shoulder. "I need to go. You need to rest and recuperate. I shouldn't be long."

Making a vow to himself to cut Ashley loose, or at the very least to be honest about his non-intentions, he backed the truck down the drive, knowing even as he made the vow he'd break it. He needed her right now. The rest would sort itself out.

No, Sawyer, she wants a ring and a baby.

He sighed, waiting for the light to change, realizing that the sort itself out bit was about to lead him straight back to husband and fatherhood with another woman he didn't truly love.

He found Miranda's house, a modest but best he could tell in the deluge, charming, thirties-era two story A-frame on a corner lot. Grabbing his toolbox from the back he ran to the front door, getting drenched in the process. The wooden door opened and he stepped into a small foyer that opened into a living room. He recognized her leather couch and chair, and the chaos of blankets and laptop. He narrowed his eyes at a pile of unfamiliar items on the rug. Things that looked like toys.

"Hi," a small voice said somewhere near his knees.

He looked down, rain dripping onto the gleaming hardwood floors and saw a little boy with sandy blond hair and huge green eyes. He was holding out his hand. "I'm Harry," he said.

"Sawyer," Miranda yelled from somewhere under his feet. "That you? I'm down here!"

He moved past the kid, not taking his hand, not understanding any of this, until he found the kitchen and steps to the basement. A horrific smell hit his nose as he started down. When he landed in the near foot of smelly water and saw her trying to use a snake on the floor drain, he ran to her and grabbed it out of her hands. As he turned the crank faster and she stepped back, he felt something catch, then give way. Water started draining, leaving behind a nasty sludge on the concrete floor.

"Gross," she said, shuddering at the mess.

"I thought you had water coming in from a downspout," he said, not looking at her.

"I did, over there," she said, pointing to the corner of the basement where water was still oozing through a small window. "That's your next job."

"I'll need a shovel," he said, heading back up the steps. "Sorry, but your floors are gonna be nasty up here for a while too."

"Go out the back," she said. "There's a shovel leaning against the garage."

Ten minutes later he'd diverted the pool of standing water away from the low place near the window with a quickly dug trench. He was also soaked to his skin. He looked up to see the little boy staring at him out the window. When their eyes met, the kid disappeared.

He made his way back around to the kitchen door and stepped inside. "Here," Miranda said, handing him a towel.

"This isn't gonna cut it, sorry. I need a shower. I'm covered in mud and smell like—" He stopped when he saw the boy standing in the kitchen looking both worried and protective.

"Fine," she said, pushing her hair off her forehead. "Harrison, show Mr. Callahan where the bathroom is, after he strips out of his shoes and clothes."

Sawyer frowned.

She smiled at him and his pulse raced in a way that it never did around Ashley. "Go on, I'm not looking, don't worry." She turned to the stove and put a teapot on a burner. Sawyer glanced down at Harrison, or Harry, or whoever he was, although he knew damn good and well this was the "baby" he'd asked about that fateful day in her condo. He shucked out of his boots and drenched clothes, leaving them in a pile by the back door, wrapped the towel around his waist and followed the stern-looking kid to the bathroom.

"Here," the boy said, pointing to the shower.

"Thanks," Sawyer said. Harrison studied him for nearly a minute, his eyes dark, his brow furrowed. Finally, he ducked out the door, hollering for his mother.

Chapter Nineteen

A few weeks after the rain disaster, Sawyer and Ashley sat on Miranda's couch, watching the football game while Miranda flirted with the guy she was dating and Harry bounced around in front of the television, his eyes darting from his mother to Sawyer and back again. They'd settled into a nice, friendly routine since the night of the backed-up sewer. Sawyer took the kid to the Y to swim once a week, and they'd go out for "man burgers" afterwards. Harrison claimed that the only person he ever wanted to play cards with ever again in his whole life was Emma. They all hung out together, and it was, if not always comfortable, at least not awkward.

At the moment, Sawyer didn't much care for the tool Miranda was seeing. He was a banker—one of Sawyer's least favorite people—and he tried too hard to get Harry to like him, with his blustery, fake "kiddos" and hair tousling bullshit. Sawyer knew Harry well by now. He appreciated his quietness laced with energetic outbursts, typically as related to either football or the swimming pool. The boy was a born athlete, and he'd been trying to convince Miranda to let him join the pee wee football league, so he could learn some of the rules.

He frowned when the banker grabbed Miranda's arm as she passed by him on her way back from the kitchen, dragged her down into his lap and kissed her, his hand tucked between her thighs in a way that told the full story about their level of intimacy. Ashley snuggled in closer under his arm, almost making him forget their argument that morning. She'd brought up the kid thing again. She claimed she'd be willing to forgo the marriage bit, if she could just have his baby. He'd reminded her that topic was off the table and left the room, utilizing his new arguing technique—ignore and conquer. It helped him also ignore the fact that he still hadn't properly dealt with the truckload of guilt he hauled around relative to Emma and her accident. But he'd be damned if he'd pay a shrink to help him do that. He'd sort it out his own way, eventually.

He glanced over and caught Miranda looking at him. He cocked an eyebrow. She stuck out her tongue at him, then turned her attention to the banker. Sawyer sighed and got up. "Come on, Harry," he said, grabbing the kid's ball. "Let's go throw a few."

After about fifteen minutes, Ashley emerged from the house. "Gotta go, babe," she said. "Out-of-town buyers, remember?"

Sawyer flung the football in her direction. She squealed and ducked, then got in her car. Harry ran after the ball and tossed it back to him. "I like her," he said unconvincingly.

"Yeah, me too," he said, meaning it. There was nothing wrong with Ashley other than the fact that she wasn't Miranda.

This is quite the mess you've gotten yourself into, Callahan. Quite the mess indeed.

They tossed the ball a few more minutes, then Harry asked if they could work on the tree house. They'd started the project the weekend before, which had sent Ashley off on a bit of a tear.

"You act like he's your son or something," she'd said, pouting as she sipped her wine the night after he'd spent an entire day engineering the thing, then shopping for all the wood and nails and other supplies. "It's weird."

He'd ignored her. She dropped the subject. When Emma had said more or less the same thing, he'd not been able to ignore her.

"I'm not jealous, Daddy-o, don't worry. But Ashley is. So I'm back to you needing to either tell her the truth about how you feel about Miranda or stop going over to Miranda's house so damn much."

"You're right," he said.

"I know I am. Hand me that, will you?" She pointed to the walker. It was the only device she needed to move around these days. She'd dedicated herself to physical therapy with the sort of vengeance Sawyer knew she came by honestly. He averted his gaze from her thin legs as she swung around to the side of the bed. He positioned the walker in front of her. "Gotta get my steps in." He reached for her arm, but she flinched away from him. "On my own, remember?"

"Yeah, I remember." His throat closed up the way it always did when he watched her struggle to her feet. The scar that now ran from the left side of her lips to her temple was both nasty and something she swore she didn't want to have surgery to hide. He sucked in a breath. His baby girl was alive. She was going to be fine, eventually.

But would he ever recover from it?

"Hey, Sawyer?" Harrison snapped his fingers in front of Sawyer's face.

"Sorry. Let me just grab some water. Go on back and get our tools ready."

He still had nightmares about Emma and blamed himself daily for what happened to her, so maybe this whole pretending to be Harrison's dad thing wasn't a good idea. But Miranda didn't mind. They were still friends, after all.

He downed some water and then headed toward the bathroom. When he realized the television was playing to an empty living room, he turned it off, ignoring the fact that Miranda was nowhere to be seen.

"Sawyer!" The boy's voice cut through the house. "Where are you?"

Sawyer turned. Miranda was looking right at him from the doorway to the hall. The banker was behind her, looking disheveled in a way Sawyer recognized. She frowned and breezed past him on her way to the kitchen.

"What's up?" she said, her voice only a little shaky. Sawyer followed her, stunned and shocked that he was even shocked or stunned.

"We were gonna work on the tree house," the boy was saying from the back door.

"Um, I need to go, pal," Sawyer said as he walked past them both.

"But why?" Harry's voice had a distinct, oncoming temper tantrum edge to it.

Sawyer turned. Miranda and her son were in the door. She was glaring at him. Her hair was messy and her color high in a way that socked him in right in the gut. He looked away. "Don't go," Harry called to him.

"Sorry," he said. "I'll be back." But as he climbed into his truck, he knew he wouldn't. He'd entertained this strange, unrealistic fantasy for over a month—that of Miranda and Harry and he as friend and helper, and her as, what? Celibate?

Dear Lord Sawyer, just because she's revealed herself as a single mother does not change what she told you about herself. You don't even know what sort of arrangement she has with the kid's father. And for that matter, none of it is even remotely your business.

He shut his eyes for a split second, picturing that man, the person who'd fathered the boy he'd gotten way too close to. Sawyer had flattened that man with an upper cut to his gut, followed by a right hook at Helen's funeral. That move that had cost him his cop desk job. When he opened his eyes, Miranda was at the window, gesturing for him to open it. He did, but wouldn't look at her.

"What the hell, Callahan?" she said.

"Sorry," he said under his breath. "Gotta go." He revved the engine. She stepped back. He drove straight to the office where Ashley and Miranda worked and grabbed the ring box out of his glove compartment. He'd bought it the week before, but not for Ashley, he could now admit. He'd been picturing Miranda the whole time he'd picked it out and paid for it.

He was weak. He wasn't man enough for the woman he truly wanted. So, he knew what he had to do. Since Emma's horrific accident, he couldn't stand being alone anymore, not even for a few minutes. Even with her still alive and recovering in his house.

There was only one way to deal with the sum total of those facts.

He walked in, smiled at the receptionist, and headed back to Ashley's office. She was on the phone, pacing around. She smiled at him and held up a hand, indicating she'd be done in a minute. He dropped to one knee and opened the jeweler's box. She put a hand over her mouth.

"I need to call you back," she said into the phone, then put it on her desk. She flopped into her chair. He grabbed it and pulled it close, shutting the office door with one foot and shoving her skirt up, needing her body so badly his own ached from head to toe with the needing. "Sawyer," she sighed as he hooked a finger in her panties and slid them down. "I ... oh," she sighed as he dove into his favorite distraction, the square emerald surrounded by diamonds set in platinum now forgotten on the floor.

Chapter Twenty

Miranda

December

I endured the bridal shower. I even arranged an absolutely obnoxious and over the top bachelorette party. I got up, did my job, parented my son, went to bed and got up again, day after day, in a fog of disbelief and misery.

"Oh honey, you should just tell him," my mother counseled me.

"It's a little late now, mom, don't ya think?"

I'd broken up with Nick, he of the coitus interruptus that day Sawyer asked Ashley to marry him. I could barely stand to look at him anymore and what he represented to me. The memory of that moment, standing at his car window when the words, "please don't leave. I love you," were on my lips and he was already thinking about how he was going to propose to someone else.

Now, one day before the blessed matrimonial one, I sat staring out my window at a full on blizzard while Harrison whizzed around the house bouncing off walls and making me curse Sawyer even harder for cutting my needy son out of his life. I had no explanation for it and was tired of reminding him about the "Sawyer is busy with getting married" crap.

Fucking liar. He'd said he'd never marry again. Kind of like I'd said. He'd befriended my son and dumped him too, the rat bastard.

How I could possibly believe myself in love with Sawyer Callahan, after all our weird encounters, near misses, the horror of Emma's accident and near death, his discovery of my secret life as Harry's mom. I didn't love him. But, yet, I did. I'd only ever loved one man before this, and I knew the symptoms.

Best get over it, I thought. Because he's about to marry your best friend.

I sighed and slid further down into my chair, pulling my sweater tighter around me. Anger hovered ever present. I was sick of it. I needed to go out, to drink, to pick up a man, to get laid. I could feel the urge shimmering around the edges of the anger, needling me.

I didn't go out much when I was with Harry, and now that it was permanent, I'd tried to find a guy who'd stick. I thought Nick might be that guy and he was all right, but Harry didn't like him. Plus, I couldn't stand the sight of him after that day Sawyer had practically caught us screwing.

Harry welcomed the delivery pizza and came running into the kitchen with the box to tell me that his favorite sitter, who also happened to be Sawyer's daughter, was here, too. I tried not to rush to the door, since I knew Emma couldn't drive herself yet. She only needed a cane now, which was, Neil had told me, nothing short of a miracle.

"She's got her mother's stubbornness and her father's determination. The docs are amazed at her progress."

The girl smiled at Harrison, who stood next to me, quivering in excitement, still clutching the pizza box. "Hey buddy," she said, when he wrapped himself around one of her legs. She glanced over at me. "Need me to stay over?"

"Oh, no, that's okay. It's too much for you."

"No, it's fine. I know you wanted to have some quality time with my future step mommy." She smiled, but it didn't reach her eyes.

I stuck my feet into boots, swiped on lipstick and picked up my son, turning him upside down and kissing his warm belly. "I love you Harrison," I said.

"How much?" he demanded, as if that could be quantified.

"As high as the moon, as deep as the sea," I reminded him, tickling him and then handing him over to the girl he adored almost as much as he did Sawyer. She handed him a slice of pizza, then pointed to the kitchen.

"Could we talk before you leave?"

"I should get going."

Emma frowned at me.

"Sure. Yes. Okay."

"Start the movie, Harry, I'll be right back," she said, handing my son the remote before following me to the kitchen.

I poured myself a glass of water by way of stalling, then turned to face her. She sat at the kitchen table, her Callahan stubborn face making my throat close up in advance of what I expected her to say.

"I don't know how to say this, so I'm going to start with the facts," Emma began. She reached back to fix her messy pony tail, and I had to press my fingernails into my palm to keep from helping her. She hated for anyone to think she needed help. "My dad is only marrying Ashley so he won't have to think about how miserable he is without you."

Some of the water went down my windpipe, making me splutter and choke. Emma waited me out until I could breathe and speak again. "No, I think he loves her."

"Oh, I have no doubt that he loves a lot of things about her. She's pretty and nice. She's also a good cook."

I raised my eyebrows, waiting.

"But she's not you, Miranda. You and my dad are..." She waved her hands around. "You're the fucking perfect couple."

I sighed and slumped against the countertop. "It's a little late to decide this now, don't you think?"

"He's home by himself. Right now. Go there and tell him how you feel."

I frowned at this presumptuous, but spot on, assessment of my feelings. "Sorry, but that's inappropriate and a total breaking of girlfriend code. Ashley is pretty and nice and a good cook, and one of my best friends in the world. I would never do that to her. She wants to marry your dad. He asked her to do that very thing. It's not for you or me to get into the middle of it. Now, I really have to go."

I could see the tears standing in the young woman's eyes. Now she looked like a little girl—a girl who'd almost died and was willing herself back to a normal life, one brutal physical therapy appointment at a time. "Oh honey, I'm sorry." I pulled a seat up in front of her and brushed a lock of hair out of her face. "Don't cry."

"I'm not sad. I'm furious." She swiped at her tears. "My stupid father won't stop feeling guilty about my accident. It was my fault. I shouldn't have gotten in the car with Jen that day. I knew she was a bad driver. I should've been paying attention. But she... sh-sh-she..." She was full on sobbing now. I pulled her into my arms. "She's dead," the girl sobbed as if she were just now realizing it. "My f-f-f-friend is d-d-d-dead."

"Sh, Emma. It's okay. You're okay. Cry it out, baby." I patted her back while she dampened my blouse a few more minutes before sitting up and sniffling. I pressed my palm to her cheek. "Are you seeing a therapist?"

"Yeah, it's one of my many weekly appointments. My dad won't go, though. He's so stubborn."

"And cheap," we said in unison, making her giggle and me blush.

"I know," I said, even as my mind reeled with the things she'd said to me. I glanced at my watch. "I really do have to go."

Emma grabbed my hand. "Please go talk to him? You don't have to...I mean, I think he needs someone, not my Aunt Laura and not Neil, to talk to and you guys, well, you're still friends, right?" She looked at me, hope in her damp eyes.

I squeezed her hand. "Yes. We are. And I will. You sure you're okay here? Even overnight if I stay with Ashley?"

"Yeah, I'm fine. We'll be fine. Harrison's in good hands, I promise."

"I know he is." I rose and held out my hand. I knew Emma resisted help with even something this simple. Ashley had told me it frustrated both her and Sawyer. Emma smiled, put her hand in mine, and let me help her to her feet.

Harrison was on his second pizza slice by the time we got back to the living room. I grabbed my overnight bag and kissed him again.

"Bye, mom," he said without looking at me.

I pointed my car downtown, then stopped and made an abrupt U-turn. I sat in Sawyer's driveway for a few minutes, watching his shadow pass back and forth in the large picture window. Flames threw light from the fireplace around the room. I sighed and put the car in reverse.

A knock at my window as I was looking over my shoulder made me yelp and almost run over his feet. He held up a bottle of Jefferson Reserve bourbon and smiled. I turned off the car and got out, following him into his warm, empty house.

After I left my snowy boots on a mat at the back door, we sat at his kitchen table, sipping and not talking. When we started our second drink, he got up and threw more wood on the fire, then padded back across the Turkish rug to me, letting his hand drop onto my shoulder as he passed. I shut my eyes and knocked back the booze.

"I want to tell you the rest," I said once he sat down. "I'm not sure why. Other than the fact that I..." I stopped, my throat clicking as I stopped myself from saying the worst possible thing you could to a man about to marry your friend. "Anyway," I went on, composing myself. "Here goes." Without thinking, I put my feet on his lap.

He dropped a hand to my foot and rubbed gently, his smile widening in that slow, beautiful way. I told him the rest of my story, all the way up to and including my late life pregnancy, and Harrison's messy, scary, somewhat early birth with my mother by my side. "She took him from me," I choked out. "Like we'd arranged. She wanted to. She insisted on it and, like the selfish cow I was, I let her. I let her raise my baby as if I were some teenaged mom. I visited him twice a year, over in Grand Rapids, but that was it."

I sighed and pushed my glass across the table. He re-filled it.

"He looked so much like his father." I sipped, hearing how utterly lame this story was, despite all the truth in it. "We always said once he was old enough to go to school, I'd take him. We'd live here in Ann Arbor. So, here we are. He barely knows me. His father won't acknowledge him. He misses his Nana. I hate myself. And I... I think I love you. So you abandoning him was extra shitty. But me not raising him like I should have from birth is even worse. So I guess we're even in the Harrison department."

I stuck my nose down into my glass, embarrassed beyond words. He sighed and sipped, then shoved my feet off his lap. I sat up straighter, knowing I'd said the words I'd come here to say. "I should go," I said.

Sawyer glared at me. "Your ex-husband, Trevor Landon, and Helen, my dead wife, had an affair. It went on for a couple of years. They kept at it even as she was dying at home while I took care of her, even though at the end it was only online or via some text app she had password protected on her phone."

I sucked in a breath. My heartbeat was so loud in my ears I heard nothing but it and the sound of Sawyer's breathing. He grabbed my hand, crushing it between his. "I hated her by then," he said, talking fast now. "We hated each other I guess is more like it. We should never have married. She wanted an abortion when she found out she was pregnant with Emma. I insisted we do the right thing, or what I thought was the right thing. I convinced her to marry me, to have the baby." He closed his eyes. Tears leaked out of the corners of them. Unable to stop myself, I reached out and touched his face. He shook his head. His blue eyes sparkled with more emotion than I could account for when he opened them again.

"Helen was wild. I mean, she really liked kinky stuff. And when we stopped having sex a few months before she got her diagnosis, I knew she was having it off with someone. The woman would not go without. I could barely keep up with her most of the time. But by then I didn't care anymore." He kept my hand in a death grip. "I was tuned out. Dialed in only for my daughter and my jobs." He stopped and took a breath.

"I made her go to the doctor. She had a bunch of tests. Then, one night, I came in from teaching and she was sitting in the living room in the dark. 'I'm dying, Sawyer,' she said to me."

She went fast. Pancreatic cancer is a fast moving, painful bitch. But she refused to go to a hospital. So I took care of her in our home. Nurses came to give her chemo for a week, then she refused to take it since we knew it wasn't going to help. Emma was freaked out. Reality was like some kind of strange, daily nightmare." He ran a hand around the back of his head, then grabbed the bourbon bottle and drank straight from it before setting it down with a clunk.

"You don't have to tell me," I whispered, reaching out to put my hand alongside his newly growing beard. It was coming in much lighter this time, I noticed. "It's all right," I heard myself soothing.

He shook off my hand again and got up, dragging his fingers through his hair. "She had women come in, some friends, some strangers to me." He gulped and glared down at me. "She wanted me to have sex with them in front of her. She felt bad, she said, for all our time apart before then and now that she was dying she wanted to make sure I was 'taken care of,'" he said, hooking his fingers around the words. "I refused. At least at first."

He shut his eyes and stumbled backwards. I got up and grabbed his arm before he fell over. "Then, I didn't refuse. I didn't refuse a lot." He clutched my arms and glared into my eyes. "I fucked a dozen women, two dozen maybe, in my bedroom in front of my dying wife. Sometimes with our daughter just down the hall in her room." He dropped to his knees, hands over his face.

Without thinking about it, I mirrored him. On my knees in front of him, I wrapped my arms around him, not letting go even when he stiffened and tried to pull away. "Sh," I said, closing my eyes and loving his warmth, his breath on my neck, his arms around me. We rocked back and forth a few minutes, then he let go and dropped back onto his butt. I stayed on my knees, not wanting to hear the end of this, but knowing I had to.

He swiped at his eyes in a gesture that reminded me of Emma. "She died while I held her in my arms. Like my daughter almost did. Like I almost let those fucking doctors talk me into." His brow knitted and his eyes watered. "Laura came and helped me make arrangements. I was catatonic. Not from her passing, but from how I'd behaved, how I'd let her manipulate me into acting like a depraved idiot. Before her service, I opened her laptop, not really thinking much about it. It was open to a long email conversation string between her." He glared at me. "And your ex-husband. He was your ex by then. He never used your name. He did say that his ex-wife took his child away from him." He sighed and fell all the way onto his back, his arms spread wide on the carpet, as if being crucified. "The day of the memorial, he had the unmitigated balls to show up. I decked him, then punched him at least three times after that. My cop friends had to pull me off him."

"They'd been having the affair well before your divorce was final. Hell, before you even asked for a divorce," he said, his voice soft but matter-of-fact. I was frozen, still on my knees, my head swimming with all this new information. "She loved him, she claimed. He understood her, she said. I was..." He stopped. I got up and grabbed the bourbon bottle, then sat near his head, my back propped against the wall.

I took a couple of long drinks, then handed the bottle to him. He sat up and stared down at it. "I was a dumb cop. She never should have married me. All of this she said in messages to Trevor Landon." He sucked back a long drink. "I loved her, I swear I did." He chuckled, but the sound was not pleasant at all. "Lost my dumb cop desk job after I laid him out at her funeral. But I'd do it again."

He got up and held out a hand. I let him pull me up. But instead of pulling me all the way into his arms like I wanted him to, he let go and stumbled into the kitchen. I found him staring at the sink, head down, visibly trembling.

"Why won't you cry, Sawyer," I asked him, sliding my hand up his back, his neck and into his hair. My heart ached for him. I wanted to enfold him, to protect him, to make him love me and trust me. I had never in my life wanted something so much. I hurt from head to toe with this wanting of a thing I simply could not have.

He turned his face to glare at me out of those compelling blue eyes that I hadn't been able to forget since the first time I saw them. "I don't need to." His jaw was clenched. I touched it. "Don't," he said trying to jerk out of my reach. "I can't..."

"You can't what?" I put my head on his shoulder and my arm around his waist. I didn't want anything more than to provide comfort, a safe place, so he could cope with all the shit he was hauling around.

He turned to me slowly, pressed his face into my hair, and sighed. "It's all right," I said into his chest. "I'm here."

He was shaking in my arms and for a minute I didn't understand it for what it was. When I realized his entire body was heaving with sobs, I held on tighter. And shed a few tears of my own.

We made it to the couch in each other's arms, kissing slowly, letting it build in a way I'd forgotten was pleasurable as attached to the wham-bam as I'd gotten in the last few years. But we broke away from each other before going any further.

"I won't do this to my friend," I said, getting up. "I may be easy, but I won't be the other woman, especially not to her. She deserves better from both of us."

"You're right. I'm sorry. I'll tell her."

"No, don't," I said. "It's just between us. One last kiss and all that."

He blew out a breath and sat, sprawled and tempting. I shook my head. "Get up and walk me out. Last I checked, you have but a few more hours as a single man."

He rose, draping his arm around my shoulders. It made my head pound. I leaned into him, turning at the last minute once my boots were back on and kissing him hard, tasting as much as I could, letting him press me up against the wall, hands holding my face, leaving us both breathless.

I broke away, tears streaming down my face at my inability to close this deal. "I do love you," I whispered. "I hate myself for it. But I hate myself for a lot of things, so you're going to have to take a number."

He leaned his forehead against mine. "I'm going to fix this," he said.

"Don't hurt her. She's a good person. She'll be a great wife and mom. You do know that's next on her list, right?"

He stepped back from me. "I'll make it right, Miranda. All of it."

"Oh, Sawyer. You can't fix everything with your spreadsheets and tool box, as impressive as I'm sure it is." I grinned when he blushed. "No, you go and marry Ashley. She'll be great for you. You guys will be great together."

And they would be. They both wanted something like this, something normal and stable. They both wanted it so desperately I knew they'd make it work. "Forget about me. But don't ignore Harrison, okay?" I put my hand on the doorknob, already shaking with cold and frustration, but knowing this for one of the most right things I'd ever done. "I'll be fine," I whispered into the cold, snowy air.

I looked back once. I probably shouldn't have, because when I saw him standing there, slump shouldered, blue eyes shining, looking lost and broken, I almost went back inside and took him to bed.

Almost.

Chapter Twenty-one

I sent Emma home, telling her that we'd decided to make it an early night and fell into a restless sleep. When I climbed out of bed early the next morning, I checked in on Harrison who was snoozing away, then peeked out the window. Blinking fast, I realized I was looking at my friend Ashley, standing there shivering in the snow and wearing her expensive designer wedding gown. Fussing and clucking, I pulled her inside, wrapped her in a blanket and got her some tea, terrified she'd found out that I'd gone to Sawyer's the night before even though we hadn't done anything other than cry a lot and kiss a little.

"I can't do it," she sniffled, staring into her tea. "I can't marry him."

"Okay," I said, settling into the couch. "Why not?"

"I don't love him," she said, setting her tea mug on the coffee table. "And you do."

I choked on a gulp of burning hot liquid. My vision swam and my heart pounded. "Don't be silly," I said, waving a hand in front of my face. But she didn't move. "It's not... we... didn't do anything. I swear it Ashley."

"I know that," she said, getting up to pace, dripping melting snow all over my floor. "I trust you. I told him that too, about an hour ago." She sniffled and looked down at her dress. "I wanted to wear this." She ran her hands down the front of the tight-fitting bodice. "And this." She held out her left hand, slid the ring off, and put it on the table between us. "But it should be yours."

"Don't be ridiculous," I said, my pulse racing so fast I thought I might pass out if I tried to stand.

"He's at the church right now," she said, tilting her head to one side. "Waiting."

"Then we need to get you out of this funk, sister, and over to the altar."

"He's not waiting for me. Do you still have that cream sheath? The one we bought when we were in Paris?"

I stared at her as she ran into my bedroom. "Harry, hop up, dude. Mama needs you today," she called into my son's bedroom.

He emerged, rubbing his eyes. "Why?" he asked, watching as Ashley ran back out and shoved the Dior dress into my hands. His eyes narrowed.

"Mama's getting married," I said, in wonder at myself.

"I thought Sawyer was getting married," he said, crossing his arms, looking put out and confused.

"He is," I said with a smile. "To me."

· · · ·

IT WAS FITTING AND perfect that the very people I would have invited, Ashley had invited, up to and including my mother who sat near the front, tears streaming down her face when I arrived holding Ashley's bouquet, wearing Ashley's ring and marrying the man who was not Ashley's fiancé anymore.

He grabbed onto me when I finally made it to the front. "You sure?" he asked, his blue eyes anxious.

"Never more so. Can we get on with this? I'd like to get to the wedding night part."

He grinned, nodded to the minister and in fifteen minutes, we were both on our second marriages.

The reception was a blur. I drank and ate, danced and cried and just as we were wrapping it up a few hours early, both of us eager to get in each other's arms, I saw Ashley, flirting her ever loving ass off with some guy in a tux. I sidled over to her, tipsy, bordering on drunk. "Who is that?" I asked, when he walked away, admiring the way he filled out his monkey suit.

"Paulo," she said, dreamily. "He owns his own website and graphic design company." I narrowed my eyes at her. "What? He does catering to make extra money. Lucky for me. Have a great night." She pecked my cheek. "I'm gonna too!" She scurried after the web designer slash caterer.

An arm encircled my waist and a small hand slid into mine. "Mommy," Harrison said when Sawyer picked him up so he was on our eye level. "I like him," he said, putting has palms against my new husband's bearded cheeks.

"Good," I said to my son. "Me too."

"Okay, mister, let's go," my mother said, swooping in and grabbing her delighted grandson. "Ready for a weekend at Nana's?"

"Yay!" He blurted out before leaning over to kiss my cheek, then Sawyer's.

Emma joined us, all dressed up with flowers on her cane. She slid one arm around my waist, then dropped her cane so she could pull her father close to her other side. "So is it Step Monster or Step Mommy?"

"How about Miranda?"

"That works." She kissed both of our cheeks. "Go on, get out of here. It's pretty obvious you're done with this crowd."

Sawyer glanced at me over his daughter's head. "You'll be okay?"

"Of course she will be," my mom said, holding my yawning son's hand. "She's coming with us."

Emma shrugged. "She's pretty convincing."

We laughed. I tried not to wake up from this dream I was having.

We stood, watching the room empty, holding hands. Then I turned to him and pulled his face close to mine, pressing our foreheads together. "You are going back to therapy. There's still too much you haven't dealt with." He cupped the back of my neck, closed his eyes and kissed me, reminding me of the task at hand once again. "Let's go," I said.

But leave it to Neil Jensen to keep me from my man, I figured as we hauled him into our departing limo after some kind of altercation with one of the guests. I had to shoo him away from harassing a new agent in my office, Chloe, in the meantime which set up a bit of a clamor of panic in my brain. Chloe was one of the sweetest, most innocent souls I'd ever encountered. I was not about to let Neil do anything to or with her, regardless of how star-struck the poor girl seemed to be as the driver pulled out into the slushy street, heading for the nearest hospital.

"Dumping you off, buddy," my new hubby said, patting the man's leg. Neil groaned. "You'll be alright, won't you?"

"Jesus, hon, he looks awful," I said, resting my hand on Sawyer's thigh.

"He's fine. Aren't you?" He glared at Neil.

"Yeah, I'm fine. But I am gonna puke."

I yelped and shifted out of his way so he could hit the window down button and lean out. "What happened," I asked in a whisper. Sawyer threaded his fingers in mine and kissed my knuckles.

"Unhappy husband is my guess."

"Unhappy...oh...," I said, as it sunk in. "Really?"

"Yeah. Really."

"Well, thank god I told him to steer clear of my new agent. He looked a little predatory around her earlier."

Neil slumped back into the seat, wiping his lips as the cold snowy air swirled into the limo, making me shiver. "Sorry," he said.

Sawyer handed him a bottle of water and a paper towel. "Apology accepted," he said. "Oh, and here we are. Out you get. I have an agenda to get to. I'm sure you understand."

We pulled up in front of the emergency department doors. Neil gave a weak salute and tumbled out into the snow. We waited until he made it inside before Sawyer told the driver to leave.

Once we were checked in, the hastily packed luggage already delivered to a local hotel, our ostensible honeymoon locale until we figured out a way to take a real vacation, we stood, looking at each other for a few seconds. Then he tugged off his tie, shucked his dark jacket and held out his arms. I went into them, letting him hold me so close I heard his heartbeat in my ears for days after that.

"I want to make love to you the rest of my life, Miranda," he whispered as he slid the zipper down on the back of my dress. We let it pool on the floor at my feet. "That work for you?"

"I'm counting on it, actually," I said, pretending to look stern.

The room faded as he laid me back on the bed and kissed his way from my earlobes to my toes, paying extra attention to several more sensitive places in between. He was about to make me climax with his lips and tongue—the way I'd told him was required once, at a local bar, over too much bourbon. "Stop," I said, my voice rough. "Come up here." I tugged at his arms. I wanted this, but I wanted him inside me, sharing the moment, for our first time. He rose from between my legs, his lips wet and his eyes shining.

"Clothes off," I said, pointing at his crotch. "Bring that here."

"Yes ma'am," my husband said, unbuckling his belt in a way that ought to be illegal, his gaze never leaving mine. He stood before me, naked, his body imperfect and perfect at the same time. I crooked my finger at him.

"Closer," I said. "I won't bite."

"I know," he said in a whisper. "I'm just making sure I'm not dreaming this."

"You're not. Let me show you how real I am." I pulled him to the bed, pushed his shoulder so he was on his back, and straddled his hips, taking him deep inside me so fast we both gasped. "Oh yes," I said, dropping over him. "That's more like it."

"Is it?" he said, smiling up at me.

"Oh yeah," I said. "It most definitely is."

We let the real world drop away, and when we checked out and went to his truck, I said, "What day is it anyway? And by the way, where are we going to live?"

He laughed and pointed the car toward my house. "Wherever you are, is where I'll be."

"God damn Callahan, did you take romance novel dialogue lessons or what?"

I smacked the inside of his thigh. He grabbed my hand and moved it higher. I leaned over to kiss him, already memorizing his taste and feel and wanting more. "I want you in my bed tonight," he said with a low growl.

"I'm game," I said, pulling away and patting my hair primly. "Harrison's good until Tuesday."

Chapter Twenty-two

S awyer
A few months later

"Emma, are you up?"

Sawyer called up the steps after getting Harrison onto the school bus. He skirted the plastic sheeting covering the open back wall of the house, cursing the subs for being late or non-existent. He could've had the damn addition framed, dry walled and painted himself by now and for a hell of a lot less money.

"I am so late," Miranda said, scurrying around the temporary kitchen. They were making do with an electric cook top, coffee maker, and mini fridge set up in what was the living room while the back half of their house was demolished and put back together again. He watched her, admiring her in her short work skirt, the long line of her neck, the way she flushed red when she fanned her face with a file. The a/c was out while the house was under re-construction and it was a freakish nearly ninety degrees this first week of October.

Her hormones were roiling post-surgery, but it was the best he could do, since every decent contractor in a fifty-mile radius had been booked up for months once they'd decided to make the renovations to this house. He and Neil had done all the demo, with help from a couple of his stronger kids. An emergency hysterectomy hadn't been in the plan, but when it had become obvious that she was miserable and her gynecologist had suggested it as a solution, they'd gone with it. Which meant he'd turned the reconstruction over to a builder so he could focus on helping her recover.

"I hate you right now," she said, glaring at him and blowing a lock of hair out of her eyes.

"I love you too, dear," he said, pouring himself a cup of coffee. "Wait, don't go away mad," he said, grabbing her and sliding his hand up that tempting swath of black sheathing her ass. "Can I? Can we?"

he asked, cupping her breast and sensing her breathing get faster. He slanted his lips over hers, loving the way she kissed him back.

"Sorry, no time. I need to go sell a few houses to support this boondoggle life we have," she said, breaking the kiss with a smile. His heart gave a firm thump in his chest, reminding him how happy he was. "But we could do this." She glanced around him to make sure Emma wasn't on the steps, then tugged his sweat pants down and gripped his hard cock.

"Nope," he growled, yanking her back up before she dropped to her knees. "I'm a big boy. I can wait." He cupped her chin in one hand. "I love you, wife."

She gave his dick one last lovely stroke, then pulled his sweats back up. He patted her ass. He could never get enough of his wife. They'd gone without sex out of medical necessity for several weeks and had enjoyed falling back into each other's arms since getting the green light from her doctor.

"God, I'm hot." She swiped sweat from her upper lip. "Sometimes I wonder if that procedure did me any good at all."

"Yes, you're hot. And yes, it did." He gave her butt one more admiring pat before turning to greet his grumpy daughter, and the lazy sons of bitches who were supposed to be renovating his house.

"Morning, Emma."

"Morning, Step Monster," she said, yawning and pouring herself a cup of coffee. "Father," she said.

"Did you get those applications finished?"

"'Finished and sent. Why? You that eager to get rid of me?"

Sawyer pulled her close under one arm and grabbed Miranda on her way past him under the other. "My women," he said, kissing their hair before letting them go.

"Ew, Dad. How patriarchal. I'm not your chattel. Am I right, Miranda?"

"Definitely," she said.

"Yoo hoo," a voice floated through the house.

"That's my ride," Miranda said.

"Hey Ashley," Emma said. "How's the bump?"

"Ugh. Don't ask. God damn it, Miranda, why did you let me do this?" Ashley flopped into one of the kitchen chairs now in the living room, as the contractors began making a racket out back. She put a hand on the ledge of her pregnant belly.

"Last time I checked, you wanted that hot hubby of yours to knock you up," Miranda said. She shouldered her bag and pulled Ashley to her feet. "Let's go, baby mama. We have work to do."

Sawyer watched all of this, smiling, sipping coffee, and grateful that both he and Ashley had come to their senses. When he'd spotted Miranda at the back of the chapel the day he'd been fully expecting to marry her friend, he knew everything was going to be right in his universe.

"I love you," he called to Miranda's retreating back.

Both women waved.

"Cool. Sister wives, much?" Emma said, one dark eyebrow raised. "That would've been convenient for you."

"Spare me," he said, finishing his coffee and heading out to light a fire under the contractors. As he was standing and watching them get to work, he glanced at the text on his phone.

Miranda: *I need an expert appraisal consultation later today. Meet me at 3 at 505 Dexter Ave. Wear the grey sweat pants. You know what those do to me.*

Sawyer: *Yes Ma'am.*

Miranda: *Bring the lube.*

Sawyer: *I don't go anywhere without it.*

Miranda: *I heart emoji you. He smiled at her use of the words and not the actual little goofy symbols, because she knew he hated those damn things.*

Sawyer: *I'm going to eggplant emoji your sexy lipstick mouth emoji.*

Miranda: *That's not all you're gonna eggplant emoji. Peach emoji. Better take a pill emoji, Silver fox husband.*

Sawyer: *I'll take 2 pills for you, hot cat emoji wife.*

Miranda: *Better not. Don't want any heart attacks or anything.*

Sawyer: *Can we go back to having emoji sex talk? I don't want to be reminded how old I am. C u at 3. I'll be the dude with a hard on in grey sweats. Oh, and you can leave your panties in the car.*

Miranda: *XOXO*

Sawyer grinned, then looked up at the reconstruction project and frowned. "Hey, that's not straight. What makes you think that's straight?" He started bellowing at the subs again, but with a big smile on his face.

Chapter Twenty-three

Miranda

I sat staring at the deal, falling apart in front of my eyes on the screen. "Haley," I called, yelping when my new assistant appeared right under my elbow. "Oh crap, you are worse than Radar on MASH."

"Who?"

"Never mind," I said. "Get the bank on the phone. I need a second appraisal."

I looked up when I heard Ashley's voice. She slouched into our office looking red-faced and flustered.

"What's wrong," she asked, wincing and hanging on to her lower back.

"Nothing's wrong. I just wanted to show you how many hits this new website's getting. Your baby daddy is a damn miracle worker." I pointed to the dashboard of my new site. I had thousands of click throughs and was getting at least two emails a day, several of which I'd converted to sales.

"Glad it worked out," she said, accepting tea from Anna. "He's a miracle worker, all right."

"Oh," I asked, swiveling away from the screen and giving her my full attention. "You don't sound so certain."

"I am exhausted. I'm running on about three hours of sleep a night. It's fucking hot as hell outside. My tits are killing me I can't find a single comfortable position whether I'm sitting or laying down or..." She burst into tears. I motioned for Anna to leave and shut the door behind her.

"Hang in. It gets better," I said, handing her a tissue.

She rolled her eyes, sniffled some more, and then stood up.

"I may never have sex again," she mumbled into her tissue.

"Never say never," I said. "Go sell something. You'll feel better. Besides, you love that hot stud of a baby daddy and you know it. Hell,

I'd let him impregnate me if I hadn't relinquished my baby making parts."

She stuck her tongue out at me, gave me a quick hug, then headed down the hall.

My computer bleeped with an incoming video message. I opened it up and settled myself in for a long argument. "You are so full of shit, it's leaking out your ears. I see it from here."

The man's face on the screen contorted into a grimace. His blue eyes sparkled with unnecessary, annoying glee. "You need people like me to keep you grounded in reality, Realtor-lady. You know that pile of crap is not worth a half a mil. Get real."

I sighed. "I found comps. I handed them to you. You didn't even have to look that far."

"Those comps were stale and one of 'em was five miles away. Please. You're losing your touch."

"No, you're a controlling jerk off determined to ruin everyone's lives by jettisoning their deals with your low-balling bullshit."

"Look, I know the market's gone crazy. I realize there are bidding wars on the crappiest of houses and that forces prices up. But I work for the lenders and it's my job to protect their investments, not make sure your latest double-dip cream puff of a deal goes through."

I ended the video chat as he was about to say something else know-it-all and bossy.

Around three o'clock, he dinged me again. I rolled my eyes and opened the screen. "What now? I'm busy trying to find some more clients since you're making my double-dip cream puff disappear like so much smoke. Where's my son?"

"He got a ride to practice. We're gonna head over there later to watch."

"I don't like him playing that game. He's not old enough."

"He'll be fine. He loves it and you know it and there's no contact for a lot of years. I made spaghetti sauce," he said. "Can you smell it?"

I grinned, so damn happy I thought I might just keel onto the floor from it. "Such a nice house husband," I said, knowing this got under his skin.

He chuckled. "As long as you leave the house for work all power suited every morning then let me fuck you in an empty house in the afternoon, you can call me the pool boy for all I care. See you soon, love."

I touched the screen with a fingertip. He did the same then ended the video call.

Later that night, after dragging Harrison away from an old movie about football, we put him to bed and headed back to the couch. I leaned on my husband's shoulder and sighed.

He kissed my hair. "What's wrong?"

"I'm too happy," I said, meaning it.

"No such thing," he declared, kissing my hand and putting it on the tent he was building under his shorts. "See? Always room for more happiness in the world."

"You're a pig," I said, feeling sleepy and content.

"No, I'm your pig," he said, cupping my breast.

Emma stomped past us at that moment. "Cut it out. You have a bedroom."

Sawyer sighed and looked at me. "Sorry. She's a teenager."

I smiled. "Yes, and one that is mere weeks away from leaving the nest for college." I let myself drift asleep while the tv droned and my husband stroked my hair. When I woke, he was sound asleep too so I kissed him awake.

"Thanks, by the way," I said as I pulled him to his feet.

"For what am I being thanked?"

Grinning at the echo of one of our long ago conversations. "For fixing it, like you said you would."

"I have a mean set of tools," he whispered into my ear, making me shiver with happiness.

"Oh yeah? Prove it, old man."

He tossed me over his shoulder and ran for the bedroom by way of an answer.

• • • •

THE END

Thanks for reading APPRAISED, a Stewart Realty Affiliated Novel. CONTINGENT, a novel about Neil, Sawyer's friend, the HandyMan Inc. guy, is coming soon.

Here's a quick peek....

The shrill alarm tone sliced through Neil's fuzziness, making him groan and roll over, scrabbling around for the pillow to drag over his head. He'd swear it was the weekend and he hadn't set any sort of alarm. The first job he'd scheduled wasn't until the afternoon, on purpose.

His hand landed on something warm and soft. It moved, which clued him in that it was definitely not his pillow. When he lifted his aching head, he had to acknowledge that he'd gone and done it again. This new habit of waking up in strange bedrooms with women he barely remembered was a bad one. Taking them to his house let him control things—he could boot them out when he was done without too much unnecessary conversation or weirdness.

"God..." he groaned when he rolled away from the warm body and put his bare feet on the strange carpet. "Double that," he said, when his brain slammed into the front of his skull too fast and the room did an alarming one-eighty on him.

That noise....what was it and why wouldn't it stop? He reached for the stack of crap on the bedside table, nearly falling off the bed in the process. Several items dropped onto the floor. He tried to focus on them, to see which one was making such a racket so he could throw it through the wall. As he was trying to figure out why there was a set of handcuffs on the floor at his feet, his memory of the night before kicked in.

"Oh shit," he muttered, deciding he should get the hell out of here before the woman woke up. Realizing they were in a casino suite in Detroit, he rose, slowly, wincing at the various pains he had in very odd places. Limping over to the black-out curtains, he shoved them apart, figuring it best, like ripping the band-aid off the wound.

The day was overcast, which was a blessing. He blinked and rubbed his face, then turned around to face the chaos surrounding the giant bed.

The horrific wah-wah-wah of the alarm had not made any sort of impact on the naked woman. So Neil made his slow way back to the bed, noting at least two discarded condoms on the floor along with the handcuffs, the lube, a set of nipple clamps and two empty bottles of champagne. A stack of casino chips perched at the edge of table on her side of the bed. Neil picked one up, palmed it and glanced over at the passed out woman. Her deep red hair was covering half her face. That had been the attraction, he knew. He had a new thing for redheads. She'd been on a winning streak, he recalled, which had caught his attention. He put the chip back and slid the sky-high black patent leather shoe with the deep red sole the rest of the way off the foot she had dangling over the edge of the bed.

She sighed and rolled to her side. The gleam of her gigantic wedding ring hit his eye, making him wince and even more eager to vacate the premises before she woke and could regale him any more about her shithead banker husband. He'd been into married women lately—the challenge of it was a buzz. The extraction was almost always easier since most of the time they were eager to get away from him and home before their hubbies showed up from the business trip or the night out with the boys or whatever.

The noise ceased, leaving a strange echo in his brain. Neil sighed and headed for the bathroom, the dual urges to pee and drink three gallons of water spurring him forward instead of backwards into the tumble of silky sheets and debauchery. Those two needs met, he decided against a hot shower in favor of a conversation-less escape. Just as he was buttoning up his shirt, the alarm, or whatever it was, started up again, making him curse and the pounding in his head ramp up.

He squinted at the pile of cords and devices still on the bedside table and finally located the culprit. His phone of all things was buzzing and screeching like a damn banshee. It was a call. Confused about when he'd set the ring tone to DEFCON One, he frowned at the name on the screen. Since when did Ashley Prine call him in the mornings? She was a real estate agent he knew from HandyMan work and she had been fun for a couple of hook-ups, but he'd sensed her innate clinginess and had put her off long enough for her to get the message.

On a whim, he'd set Sawyer up with her, just to see how they might hit it off. He knew his buddy was in a drought and needed some affirmation of his own manliness or whatever after his wife's betrayal from the grave. No better way, to Neil's mind, than to take a smoking hot chick out for an expensive dinner then straight to the sheets. If what he remembered about Ms. Prine held true, Sawyer would not be disappointed.

Neil hadn't asked about their first date but Sawyer had volunteered that he'd "enjoyed himself" and had plans to see her again.

No big surprise there. Ashley Prine was nothing if not imminently enjoyable. Neil knew this from direct experience.

So what in the hell could the woman want with him now, at – he squinted at the clock – eight in the fucking morning?

The phone squawked again, making him flinch. He put it to his ear. "What in the hell do you want?"

"Oh, God, Neil, I need you...It's Sawyer..."

Neil got up too fast, making his head swim. "What's wrong?" He was imagining mid-coitus heart attacks or strokes. "Is he okay?"

She started sobbing and sniveling.

"Calm down, Ashley. What is it? Where are you?" He'd stuffed his wallet and keys into his pockets and was halfway to the suite door before she could form a coherent sentence. He stopped cold at her words, his knees buckling so fast he tripped going up the two steps from the bedroom to the main area of the room. "I'm on my way," he said, once she'd choked out where they were. "Twenty minutes. Tell him...tell him I'm coming."

"Hurry, Neil, please? His sister's on her way too but I...don't know what to do."

"Have you called Miranda yet?" He named her friend, the super hot and awesome red-headed manager of the real estate office where she worked. She and Sawyer had been basketball playing buddies or something, at least Sawyer had mentioned her more than once to Neil which made him understand that she was likely on the man's radar as well.

"Yes. She's out in Vegas though and I can't get her yet."

"Okay, just don't leave him alone, whatever you do." He smacked the down button on the elevator and hung up on the crying woman, then sank to his heels against the back wall, willing himself able to handle what he had to face next.

Dive into the series that started it all—The Stewart Realty Series!

The books are listed in order and it's recommended that you read them that way.

Floor Time

Sweat Equity

Closing Costs

Dual Agency

Escalation Clause

Conditional Offer

Mutual Release

Good Faith **

Backup Offer

Another way to totally devour the series is by reading them in trilogies.

The Original Stewart Realty Trilogy contains Floor Time, Sweat Equity, Closing Costs.

The Forever After Trilogy contains Dual Agency, Escalation Clause, Conditional Offer

**GOOD FAITH is a novel affiliated with the series but it is not a romance. It has a lot of romantic storylines but also a fair bit of real life drama and is a great book to read before BACKUP OFFER which is a "ten years later" second generation, second chance novel.

About the author:

Liz Crowe is a Kentucky native and graduate of the University of Louisville living in South Carolina. She's spent her time as a three-continent expat trailing spouse, mom of three, real estate agent, brewery owner and bar manager, and is currently a digital marketing and fundraising consultant, in addition to being an award-winning author.

The Liz Crowe backlist has something for any reader seeking complex storylines with humor and complete casts of characters that will delight and linger in the imagination long after the book is finished.

Her favorite things to do when she's not scrolling social media for cute animal videos is walk her dogs, cuddle her cats, and watch her favorite sports teams while scrolling social media for cute animal videos.

• • • •

FOLLOW ALONG WITH LIZ online:

Lizcrowe.com

@lizcroweauthor on Facebook, Instagram, TikTok and Twitter

Don't miss out!

Visit the website below and you can sign up to receive emails whenever Liz Crowe publishes a new book. There's no charge and no obligation.

https://books2read.com/r/B-A-ZHTD-HPNED

BOOKS2READ

Connecting independent readers to independent writers.